To Reveal A Reckless Love

THE BRITISH ARE COMING
BOOK FOUR

ROBIN LEE HATCHER

Prologue

Eden's Gate Ranch, Idaho
January 1896

R oger Bernhardt stood in the parlor of the Eden's Gate ranch house, the print on the telegram blurring before his eyes, his mind refusing to believe the news. He blinked several times to clear his vision, then read it again.

PETER BERNHARDT KILLED CARRIAGE ACCIDENT LONDON TUESDAY LAST STOP.RETURN ENGLAND SOON AS POSSIBLE STOP WYMAN ACKERMAN.

Father dead? It couldn't be true. It couldn't be real.
"Roger?"
He looked up from the telegram in his hand and found William Overstreet in the doorway to the dining

room. Roger shook his head slowly, still attempting to deny the message.

"What is it?"

"It's my father," he managed at last. "He . . . he's dead."

"Good heavens, man." William took a step forward. "Was he ill?"

"No. It was an accident, according to his man of business."

"I'm sorry, Roger. What will you do now?"

Return to England was what Ackerman wanted him to do—expected him to do—and as soon as possible. It was what his father would have expected as well. But perhaps this was Roger's opportunity to do the unexpected.

Chapter One

Cinnabar, Montana
July 1896

Victoria Castleton stepped from the second-class car of the Northern Pacific Railway onto the station's platform and paused to get her bearings. It had taken nearly a week to travel across the country from Boston to this terminus a few miles outside of Gardiner, Montana. Over twenty-five hundred miles, she'd been told. But these last fifty-five miles, from Livingston to Cinnabar, had been the worst. Perhaps they'd only seemed that way because she'd known how close she was to the end.

She was tired. Her traveling dress was wrinkled. Her eyes burned from dust and soot.

Clutching her small valise—while praying her trunk would make it from the train to the stagecoach without mishap—she forced her feet to move. Her body felt uncertain without the constant sway of the train.

She followed the other passengers, and it wasn't long before she joined some of them in a stagecoach, squeezed between a portly, red-faced man on her left and a stout, gray-haired woman on her right. Across from them sat a young mother with two wailing boys—twins, by the look of them.

The final three miles into Gardiner promised to be even worse than the previous fifty-five.

When the coach jerked into motion, the children fell silent, their moist eyes growing wide. Their mother put her arms around their shoulders and drew them close to her sides.

"Have you come far?" asked the woman beside Victoria. When she didn't answer, the woman gave Victoria a nudge. "I meant you, dearie."

"Oh, I beg your pardon." Victoria glanced to the side. "Yes. From Boston."

"Mercy me. And you're traveling alone?"

"I am."

"It's a brave one, you are."

Victoria smiled briefly. "Not so very brave. But I had to come."

"Why's that?"

"I'm looking for my brother. The last I heard from him, he was in Yellowstone National Park." She looked out the window of the stage at the passing countryside. "That was nearly a year ago."

The woman released a soft gasp. "A year? Good heavens. That's a long time to go without a word."

"I wish I hadn't waited so long. But it isn't the first time I've heard nothing from him for months at a time.

He isn't a good correspondent." Of course, the same could be said of her. She hadn't written as often as she should have nor *what* she should have written. She hadn't apologized for the words she'd spoken in anger before Grayson left Boston.

"Well, I hope you find your brother and that you find him well."

"Thank you. I hope so too."

The woman seemed content to fall into silence, and Victoria was grateful. Her head throbbed, and worry for Grayson pressed heavily on her chest.

Lord. She closed her eyes. *Keep him safe wherever he is. Help me find him. Let me tell him I'm sorry.*

Her thoughts drifted backward. She pictured her younger half-brother as the two of them ran around the extensive gardens of the Castleton estate. She imagined them later, in the more modest house they'd moved to after her stepfather's financial disgrace. Memories of the two of them at their parents' funeral came next, and she felt the heartbreak anew, despite the passage of time.

"Get an education, Grayson," she'd told him countless times. *"Find a sensible way to make a living so you won't have to struggle ever again. So you'll be secure."*

But he hadn't listened to her. He'd been a boy with his head in the clouds. Always. And he'd become a man determined to chase those clouds. She could only hope and pray he hadn't stepped off the edge of the world with his eyes still fixed on the heavens.

ROGER SAT in the restaurant across the street from the hotel in Gardiner, anticipation stirring in his belly. Tomorrow a private coach would take him—and all of his art supplies—into Yellowstone National Park. For the next two months—perhaps more—he would spend every day trying to capture the beauty of the park on canvas. Two months of uninterrupted sketching and painting. Two months to do whatever he pleased.

The rattle of harness and creak of wagon wheels announced the arrival of the stagecoach from Cinnabar moments before it rolled into view, coming to a halt in front of the hotel. As Roger ate his roast beef sandwich, he watched three men unload luggage from the top and back of the coach. He knew passengers also disembarked but he couldn't see them from this side of the street. By the time the stagecoach moved on, all the passengers had entered the hotel. All but one young woman who remained on the boardwalk, a valise in one hand, a medium sized trunk at her feet. She stared down the length of the dusty thoroughfare, taking in the storefronts, the saddle horses, the wagons and buggies, and the people moving about the town.

She wasn't beautiful in the usual sense of the word —perhaps her face was too narrow, her nose too long, her chin too sharp—but something about her caught his attention, made him wish he'd brought his sketchbook with him. In fact, he wondered if he'd seen her before. He frowned. That was unlikely.

He leaned toward the window, studying her more intently. Her dark hair was caught high on her head, most of it hidden under her hat, a hat the same mauve color as her traveling dress. She was tall for a woman, and her form was without an abundance of curves, yet quite feminine at the same time. Her eyes, even from across the street, were what most caught his attention. He would very much like to see them close up. Maybe then he would understand this feeling of familiarity.

As if sensing his gaze, she looked in his direction. He doubted she could see anyone through the glass. Not with the sun at its current angle. And yet he was tempted to raise his hand to wave at her. Before he could do anything so irrational, an attendant came out of the hotel, spoke to the young woman, then lifted the trunk and carried it inside. She followed right behind him, disappearing into the shadowy interior.

Roger ate the last bite of his sandwich, then slid his now empty plate back from the edge of the table. After paying for the meal, he left the restaurant and followed the boardwalk down the length of Main Street.

It felt good to stretch his legs, perhaps more so because he knew what was ahead of him. Tomorrow he would be closed up in a coach for eight to ten hours. And the next day would be the same. The weather was good, so he wasn't worried about muddy roads causing problems. Nonetheless, he remembered the journey he'd taken the previous summer when he'd come to paint in the park. It wasn't an easy trip.

After crossing the street, Roger paused outside Henderson's Fine Fabrics, the name of the establishment painted in large letters above the door. Although the store was nowhere near as large or fine as Bernhardt & Son in London, the display in the window brought to mind his father, and he felt the sting of loss—and regret. Nothing Roger had accomplished with his art had earned a single word of praise from Peter Bernhardt, and only since his father's death had he realized the ways the old man's disapproval still wounded him.

"I wish it had been different for us," he said softly.

Taking a breath, he resumed his walk along Main Street toward the hotel. But his thoughts remained on his father.

Peter Bernhardt's tragic death had allowed Roger the freedom to remain in America beyond the one year he'd planned. There were moments when he felt a stab of guilt over the sale of Bernhardt & Son, and yet he knew he'd done the right thing, both for the company and for himself. Bernhardt's Drapery—minus the son—would continue under Wyman Ackerman's capable hand. His father's name would be remembered in London while Roger was free to live the life he wanted rather than the one so carefully planned for him by another. Now he was free to pursue his artistic endeavors wherever they led him. And tomorrow they were leading him into Yellowstone.

He slowed his steps when he saw the sign for a barbershop. As he rubbed his jaw with his right hand, he wondered if he should have his hair and beard trimmed now or wait to do so at the hotel. Through the glass he saw two men in the barber chairs and three more waiting in chairs against a wall. That made up his mind for him. He moved on.

He was almost to the hotel when the woman in the mauve gown came out the front doorway. She hesitated a moment on the boardwalk, and he stopped walking to observe her once again. Why did he feel certain he should know her? The answer eluded him as he watched her cross the street and enter the restaurant he'd vacated not twenty minutes ago.

Chapter Two

S eated in the hotel lobby the next morning, Victoria pulled the last letter she'd received from Grayson from its envelope. After unfolding the paper, she pulled the case holding her reading spectacles from her reticule, opened it, and slid the glasses onto her nose, the slender arms resting on the tops of her ears.

Over the many months since receiving the letter, she'd almost memorized it, but she reread every word of it now, all the same.

Yellowstone Lake Hotel
10 September 1895

Dearest Vicky,

I know it has been far too long since I last wrote you. There is much that I have seen and done since leaving Boston. Too much to put into letters, so I will only talk to you about where I am now.

Words are inadequate to capture the wonder I have found in Yellowstone National Park. I arrived in early August and must say that I wish I had come sooner. The hotel where I am currently residing is a vision of refined simplicity amidst nature's untamed grandeur. It stands proudly on the lakeshore, its pale walls glowing in the sunlight, the gleam softened by morning mist off the lake. The structure itself is unpretentious yet elegant, with its long colonnade of white pillars gracing the entrance. Many of the guests who stay in the hotel are wealthy. They pay little attention to someone like me. For the most part, people of more modest means make use of camps scattered around this vast park. I have done that too. But for now I am a guest of the hotel. You would love to do the same. You would enjoy visiting with all the different people coming through.

As for the lake, it stretches before the hotel in a shimmering expanse of blue, so vast and tranquil that it seems to merge with the sky at the horizon. Early in the morning, the water reflects the mountains and clouds like a mirror crafted by divine hands. By afternoon, it sparkles with the brilliance of scattered jewels. Come evening, the surface transforms into liquid fire, ablaze with the colors of the setting sun. I often sit by the shore, sketchbook in hand, marveling at the interplay of light and shadow as it dances across the water and the pine-covered slopes. It is a place of infinite inspiration, where every glance reveals a new subject worthy of capturing in charcoal or paint.

However, dear sister, you were entirely right about me. I do not have the talent required to truly capture any of it, no matter how many times I try. And I have tried. Again and again over the past couple of years. Not only in Yellowstone but everywhere I went before coming here. And I have failed. Again and again. That saddens me, for I love to draw and paint, and yet I know I will never be good enough for what I want to accomplish. It seems that my dream was never part of God's will for me. You were right to encourage me to get a better education so that I would be suited to a profession of some kind. I should have listened.

But I am not sorry my heart led me to this place. If you could only see this country with your own eyes, I know it would stir your soul as it has stirred mine. I trust my humble words and the sketches I am enclosing will serve as some consolation, although they fall far short of conveying the profound majesty around me.

I do not know for certain where I will go when I leave the park. Winter and the first snows are approaching, I am told, so I will need to say goodbye to the friends I have made during my stay at the hotel. I will write again to let you know where I go next, and I trust it will not be as long between letters as it was this time.

I pray that you are well and happy, and I continue to regret the way we parted.

Your loving brother,
BGT

Victoria blinked back tears as she removed her spectacles and returned them to the velvet-lined case. She'd crossed this great nation to find her brother. It wasn't likely that she would find him in Yellowstone. She knew that. Not all these months later. But he'd said he had friends at the hotel, and so that was where she would begin her search. With his friends.

God, help me find him. He's the only family I have left.

She felt loneliness swirl around her heart. Ever since the death of her mother and stepfather, she'd done all she could to keep her family of two together. To keep them safe. To make them secure. Oh, how she longed for security in an uncertain world. At sixteen, she'd become like a mother to fourteen-year-old Grayson. But, as much as he loved her, he'd always insisted on doing everything his own way. He hadn't listened to much of anything she'd tried to teach him through the years. His rebellion and stubbornness had led him to this park. Which had now led her here as well.

"All aboard for Yellowstone," a man called from the entrance to the hotel.

Quickly she put the letter into her reticule, rose, then took hold of her valise and carried it outside where other passengers were already climbing into the vehicle. She noticed her trunk, along with other luggage, loaded on top of the stage. She also noticed, as she drew closer, that she appeared to be the only female destined for the park. Four men were already seated inside, two facing forward and two backward, each sitting with one shoulder pressed to the side of the coach. Which meant she would be forced to sit between two of them.

The Townsend housekeeper, Mrs. O'Shea, scolded Victoria in her memory. *"Sure and begorrah! You shouldn't be traveling alone, Miss Victoria. You've a stubborn streak as long as that brother of yours, and 'tis the truth. It will not serve you well."*

At the moment, she couldn't disagree with Mrs. O'Shea.

The driver offered a hand to help her into the coach, and she settled between the two men facing forward, her valise set upon her lap. Across from her, one of the men tipped his hat. The other ignored her while staring out the coach window.

"Headed to the Lake Hotel, ma'am?" the gentleman on her right asked.

"Yes."

"Then if I may be so bold as to introduce myself, I'm John Benson. And that's my brother, George." He indicated the man who had tipped his hat. "That's where we're headed too."

"How do you do. I'm Miss Castleton."

"Are you traveling alone?" George Benson inquired.

"I hope to find my brother at the hotel. He came to the park to draw." Her answer was true, if not entirely honest.

Before anything else could be said, the coach pulled away from the hotel, jostling the passengers inside. Victoria clutched her valise close to her chest and prayed the journey would go well.

***

With multiple trunks and cases of art supplies strapped atop the privately hired coach—in addition to the luggage containing clothing and other items he might need over the next eight weeks or more—Roger climbed into the vehicle and knocked on the ceiling to let Donny Reardon, the driver, know he was settled.

"Hiya!" the man shouted to the teams of horses, and the coach jerked into action.

Roger had seen the stagecoach bound for the Yellowstone Lake Hotel depart about an hour before. He'd hoped to be on his way even before then, but one of his trunks had been missing. After a search that seemed to take forever, the trunk had been located in a storage room in the hotel, and at last they were on their way.

After acclimating himself to the rocking of the coach, he withdrew his copy of Audubon's *The Birds of America* from the carpetbag on the seat opposite him and let it open at random. It fell to the meadow lark, and he studied the yellows and the browns of the plate, the choices the artist had made with the foliage and the position of the dark nest among the green grasses. As happened so often when he looked through Audubon's book, he lost track of time and was surprised when he felt the coach slow to a halt.

"Mr. Bernhardt, we're going to rest the horses here."

Looking out the window, he realized they'd reached Mammoth Hot Springs already. As he descended from the coach, he took in the surreal landscape of cascading terraces that shimmered white and amber in the morning sunlight. Steam rose above the hot water, trickling down the mineral formations. The air was tinged with the scent of pine and sulfur.

He walked around, observing other travelers and

visitors to the hot springs who currently explored the terraces on foot or horseback. He had done the same the previous summer. But this time, he was focused on reaching the hotel on the lake. He would have many more weeks to tour the rest of the park.

It wasn't long before Donny summoned Roger with a shout. He gave one last glance toward the springs before striding to the coach so they could resume the journey.

From Mammoth Hot Springs, the road wound south through a lush forest of lodgepole pines. Interspersed on occasion were open meadows carpeted with the wildflowers of early summer. Over the next hour and a half, he caught sight of mule deer, elk, and a small herd of bison. While he made a few notations in a notebook, he made no attempt to sketch. The ride was too rough for that. Besides, there was too much beauty to be seen beyond the coach windows. As the road climbed, distant mountain ranges appeared, some of them capped with snow even though it was July.

They stopped again at the Norris Geyser Basin to swap out the teams of horses and to eat their midday meal. The change station served a thick beef stew with plenty of warm biscuits and tin cups of coffee. Roger and his driver were the only customers, but the woman who served them mentioned that the stage from Gardiner had departed no more than thirty minutes before.

After he finished eating, Roger allowed himself a little time to walk out and observe the geothermal activity—bubbling mud pots, hissing steam vents, and geysers. He'd been warned before about treading too close so he kept a healthy distance. The ground looked otherworldly, splashed with shades of white, orange, and green. He made himself a few more notes, including a reminder to ask someone what caused the colors that seemed too bright to be real.

"We'll stop one more time to rest the horses," Donny told him as they prepared to depart, "but we'll be at the Grand Canyon of the Yellowstone in about three hours. Despite all your trunks, Mr. Bernhardt, we're traveling a heap lighter than the regular stagecoach. Making good time."

Roger entered the coach with a little less enthusiasm than he had that morning. Donny seemed to think three hours wasn't long, but Roger's bones felt rattled and jarred. He would be thankful for a room and a bed before facing the final twenty-five or so miles of the trip tomorrow.

After leaving the basin, the coach descended into an open, grassy expanse dotted with elk herds. The Yellowstone River meandered lazily through the valley, reflecting the sky like a silver ribbon. The road, although rough, was level, and Roger was surprised when the horses slowed. Was it time to rest them already?

"There's trouble up ahead," Donny called down to him.

Trouble? Roger poked his head out the window. He could just see the back of a stagecoach stopped on the road ahead, leaning at an odd angle. "What is it?"

"Looks like they lost a wheel."

When the coach came to a complete stop, Roger

opened the door and hopped to the ground. That allowed him to see several passengers standing off to the side of the road while two men—they appeared to be the driver and the man who rode shotgun with him—stared at a broken wheel lying near the stagecoach.

"That doesn't look good," Donny said.

One of the coachmen looked up. "It ain't good. It's broke beyond repair, and we don't have a spare. They were supposed to replace it in Gardiner but didn't get 'round to it, I reckon."

Roger only half-listened to the men because by this time he'd noticed that the woman from yesterday was among the passengers. She wore the same mauve gown as before. She was also the only woman in the group, and he sensed her discomfort, even from where he stood.

"There's no change station until we reach the junction near the Grand Canyon," Donny said, "but we can let them know what's happened and send help back to you."

"Much obliged," the other driver answered.

Roger stepped toward them. "Mr. Reardon, there isn't room in the coach for all the passengers, but perhaps we could make space for the young woman so she doesn't have to wait here for so long."

"That's right kind of you, sir," the stagecoach driver responded. "I'm sure she'd appreciate it. We likely won't make it to the way station until well after nightfall." He turned, bumping his hat back on his head as he did so. "Miss Castleton, this here gentleman is offering you a ride in his coach. They'll send back help for the rest of us straight away."

The woman—Miss Castleton—looked at him. Her hazel eyes were even more beautiful than he'd suspected they would be. "Sir, that is very kind. But I don't wish to be of any trouble."

"No trouble, miss. I assure you."

Chapter Three

Donny Reardon steered the horses around the stagecoach with its broken wheel and urged them into a gallop a short while later.

Inside the coach, Roger sat across from his new traveling companion. Her trunk and valise were on the seat beside her. The visible tension in her shoulders, along with her downcast eyes, told him how uncomfortable she felt. More uncomfortable than she'd been with the four male passengers she'd ridden with from Gardiner? Perhaps she thought being in this coach with him was the greater of two evils. He supposed he couldn't blame her for that.

"Miss Castleton." He paused to clear his throat, giving her time to raise her eyes to meet his. "If I may introduce myself once more, as I said, I am Roger Bernhardt. I hale from London, England, but I have been in America for more than a year, most of that time spent in Idaho on a cattle ranch."

She bowed her head slightly. "Victoria Castleton. I'm from Boston."

"You have come a long way to visit this national park."

"It isn't the park I came to see."

"Truly?"

"Truly." Her lips thinned as they pressed together, as if to keep herself from saying more.

"This is my second visit in a year." He pointed toward the roof of the coach. "Perhaps you noticed how many trunks and cases I have with me. It's because I intend an extended stay. I am here to paint more of this great American wilderness in all its glory."

"You're an artist?" It wasn't surprise or curiosity in her voice. It was almost like . . . dismay? distress? discomfort? disapproval?

"Yes, I'm an artist." Strange. He'd never answered that question with such conviction before. He'd thought of himself as a merchant's son who enjoyed painting and sketching. But he'd been an artist from childhood and he was an artist now. It felt good to say it aloud.

"Is that how you make your living, Mr. Bernhardt? As an artist."

"Not yet. But I hope it will be."

She turned her gaze out the window. "Most men have established their careers long before they are your age."

He laughed, even though he doubted she'd meant to be funny. He rather thought she'd intended to insult him.

His laughter drew her eyes back to him. "Am I

wrong? Is it different in England?" Her words were as stiff as her demeanor.

"No." He subdued his smile. "You are not wrong, and it is not different. My father wished for me to follow him into the drapery business, but I was miserable at it and in it. I have loved to draw and paint from the time I was a young boy. It's all I wanted to do. Father had little patience with my artistic endeavors, as he called them, and wasn't happy when I chose to come with a friend to America so I could try to capture this amazing land on canvas." He could almost see his father, shaking his head as he stood near the pearly gates of heaven, still not understanding his son.

"Your father sounds like a sensible man."

Again, it was clear she didn't intend to amuse him. And yet he chuckled a second time. "Rather. Father was a very sensible man."

"Was?" Her expression softened.

Roger sobered as well. "He died earlier this year."

"I'm sorry for your loss."

He accepted her condolence with a nod.

"It isn't easy to lose a parent. I know."

"Your father?"

"And mother." She looked out the coach window again.

"Then I am sorry for you as well, Miss Castleton."

He remembered his own mother, as she'd been before a fever took her when he was a lad of ten. She'd been a woman full of life and laughter and had loved to see his childish drawings, praising them as if they were masterpieces, each and every one of them. If she'd lived, would she have tempered his father's disapproval of Roger's aspirations? It was a question he'd asked himself often through the years.

He turned his gaze out the opposite window, watching the countryside roll by. Was it too late for his dream to come true? Could he make a living from his art? Would others want to buy what he painted? The sale of Bernhardt & Son had given him breathing space. But it wasn't a large fortune. The money wouldn't last forever. If he couldn't sell his art, then he would need another way to earn a living.

Sebastian Whitcombe, his good friend, had taken to ranch life on Eden's Gate like a Mallard to the Thames. He'd branded cattle and spent long days in the saddle. He'd shot a grizzly bear and searched for rustlers. If Sebastian hadn't been a viscount with a future in England as the next Earl of Hooke, he would have been perfectly content to live the rest of his life as a cowboy in America.

But the ranching life wasn't for Roger any more than being a merchant in a London drapery establishment had been. So if he couldn't make it as an artist, what would he do?

"Your father sounds like a sensible man."

"And I, obviously, am not," he whispered to himself.

Victoria's mother—Claudette Monroe Castleton Townsend—had often said that God loved to laugh over His children. Well, surely the good Lord was laughing now. Only a divine joke would put Victoria into a coach with an artist, with a man who loved to do the very kind of thing that had kept Grayson from being practical and making good choices. The desire to draw the landscapes of the American West had taken her brother away from her, and because of it, she no longer knew where he was or how to find him.

Still, Roger Bernhardt had been kind. No one had forced him to make room in his private coach for her and her luggage. He could have had his driver pass them all by without a by-your-leave. But he hadn't. Instead, he'd taken pity on the lone woman passenger. It had been a gentlemanly thing to do, and she should be grateful for it. She *was* grateful for it, and she should show it.

Drawing a deep breath, she looked at the man seated opposite her. "Mr. Bernhardt, did I express my gratitude for you taking me with you to the next change station?"

He met her gaze. "You did, indeed, Miss Castleton. And it is my pleasure to do so. In fact, if I may, you are welcome to continue with me tomorrow down to the Lake Hotel. Last summer I rode in a stagecoach with five other park visitors, and I venture to say this coach offers more room and comfort than what you experienced this morning. I'm sure we could even find a way to put this excess luggage above so we have more room inside."

A desire to accept the offer surged within her. "I wouldn't want to inconvenience you, sir."

"It wouldn't be an inconvenience. We are going to the same destination, after all."

Guilt washed over her at his kindness. She hadn't been especially gracious since climbing aboard. Not from the moment he told her he'd come to the park to paint. His words had brought to mind the final argument she'd had with Grayson before he left Boston. Her brother's voice had been filled with anger and frustration. Hers had been the same. The memory of it had refueled her anger, and she'd almost released it on a perfect stranger.

"It's settled then," Roger said. "I'll see you safely to the hotel on Yellowstone Lake by tomorrow evening."

"That is very good of you." She recalled the jostling she'd taken for hours in the stagecoach, the man on her right bumping into her, then the man on the left doing the same. Over and over again. "I agree with you that I am much more comfortable in this coach than I was in the other."

He responded with a smile before looking out the window once again.

He was a handsome man, especially when he smiled like that. She'd noticed the striking blue of his eyes the first time she'd seen him, but now she realized there was more to his good looks. Most likely in his mid-thirties, he had golden blond hair and a close trimmed beard and mustache that revealed rather than disguised the pleasing curve of his mouth and strong cut of his jaw. He was tall and leanly built, but she suspected there was hidden strength beneath his well-made suit, a suit covered in a fine layer of dust, like everything else in the coach, herself included. She hadn't cared to learn anything about the four male passengers she'd journeyed with that morning. The same was not true of the man across from her now.

"Mr. Bernhardt?"

He met her gaze.

"You said you spent most of the last year on a ranch in Idaho. I am curious. What did you do there?"

He chuckled. "I learned I will never be a rancher."

"But if that's true, why were you there?"

"It's a strange story, I suppose."

"I should like to hear it if you don't mind telling it."

"As you wish." He seemed to give it some thought before he began. "My friend, Sebastian Whitcombe, the current Earl of Hooke, went to school with an American lad named William Overstreet. Despite their many differences, the two became close friends. After William finished school, he returned to America, and after a period of time in New York City, he eventually took over the running of his family's cattle ranch in Idaho. He wrote to Sebastian through the years, always encouraging him to come for a visit. And finally, after more than a decade, the trip was planned. Sebastian's sister, Amanda, joined him, and so did I. The two of them sought adventure. As for me?" He released a sigh. "I wanted to delay, if not escape, the destiny my father had planned for me since birth."

She understood his meaning. Hadn't she planned a completely different life for her brother after the deaths of their parents? Hadn't she wanted Grayson to be sensible, practical, to forge a future for himself that would provide security for himself and his future family?

"We arrived in Idaho in May of last year," Roger continued. "All of us were amazed by the vastness and variety of this land. The plains. The mountains. The rivers. The forests. We'd read about America, of course, but until it is seen with one's own eyes, one can hardly believe that what's written is completely true."

Her own journey from Massachusetts to Montana was still fresh in her mind, but the excitement in his voice magnified it all in her memory.

"We were welcomed into William's home, and Sebastian and Amanda took to ranch life as if they were born to it. Which—" He laughed. "—they certainly were not. Their privileged lives in England were nothing like what they found in Idaho. But that didn't stop them from falling in love with both America *and* Americans. Sebastian took his bride back to England as the new Countess of Hooke at the end of last summer, and Amanda married in the fall and now lives with her husband, Isaiah, in Montana. I hope to see them while I'm in Yellowstone."

"They will travel down to see you at the lake?"

"Not just to see me." Again he chuckled. "Isaiah works as a game scout in the park, catching poachers. Amanda rides with him."

Victoria felt her eyes widen in surprise.

Roger's laugh was louder this time. He pointed at her. "*Exactly* my reaction when I first learned of it. But she is happy. Happier than I've ever known her to be. Her letters make that quite clear."

Longing welled in Victoria's chest. How she envied those who knew complete happiness. She hadn't been truly happy in years. She'd done little but worry about money and about Grayson in the years since the deaths of their parents.

Roger's expression sobered. "As for me, I was prepared to return to England in the spring. However, I changed my plans after my father died. There was no longer any reason to go back."

"You have no other family? No brothers or sisters."

He shook his head. "No other family at all."

Without comment, she lowered her eyes as sadness washed over her. Was Grayson still alive or was she as alone in the world as Roger Bernhardt?

Chapter Four

The next morning, the air icy-cold, Roger was waiting by the coach when Victoria exited the rustic lodge that served travelers going in and out of the park. Other choices of accommodation included tents and small log cabins. Roger had spent the night in one of the latter.

A flicker of a smile crossed Victoria's lips when she saw him. Then, carrying her valise, she walked in his direction. The driver had managed to rearrange all the baggage so that almost everything was now on the roof or back of the coach, giving the two passengers more room in the compartment itself. Roger took her valise and assisted Victoria to her seat, then followed her inside.

"Are you ready?" He handed her a blanket to drape over her legs against the morning chill.

She nodded.

He rapped the ceiling of the coach. "Mr. Reardon, we can go."

The driver snapped his whip, and the horses jumped into action. Once the initial jerk and jostle was over and the coach settled into a rhythmic rocking, Roger leaned against the seat back and tried to mentally prepare himself for the hours ahead.

After a period of silence, Victoria said, "I didn't see the stagecoach this morning. Did they leave before us?"

"No. I spoke to the driver when I was having breakfast. It's doubtful they'll leave before noon. The repairs are taking longer than expected. They won't reach the Lake Hotel until tomorrow."

"How awful for them. And how grateful I am for your generosity."

"I assure you, Miss Castleton, it has been my pleasure. The time passes more quickly with a pleasant companion such as yourself."

With heavy canvas shades lowered over the windows, keeping out some of the cold mountain air, the compartment of the coach was bathed in shadows. Still, Roger saw the color rise in Victoria's cheeks, as if she wasn't accustomed to receiving even the mildest of compliments. He found that thought sad, indeed.

He also found himself wishing he could draw her. He would love to capture the curve of her jaw, the shape of her eyes, the arch of her brows. Her face seemed to hold secrets that begged to be uncovered, whether with a pencil and sketchpad or with paint on canvas. But since he couldn't sketch or paint in a rocking, jolting coach traveling the rough roads of the park, he would try to uncover her secrets in other ways.

"Miss Castleton, you said yesterday that you hadn't

traveled across the country to see Yellowstone. So what, may I ask, brought you to the park?"

She didn't answer at once. In fact, she was silent so long, he began to doubt she would. But at last she said, "My brother."

The answer surprised him, although he couldn't say why.

"Like you, Grayson loves to draw. He fancied himself an artist." She looked down, her hands clasped in her lap. "He wanted to see the West. To sketch it. But he . . . but I haven't heard from him since September of last year when he wrote to me from the Yellowstone Lake Hotel. I don't know if something untoward happened to him or if . . . or if he simply hasn't written because he is angry with me."

"I say. That isn't the done thing. Not to one's own sister."

She lifted her gaze to meet his. "Grayson was never a good correspondent. So it is possible that he's simply not gotten around to writing. We didn't part on the best of terms. Our words to each other before he left Boston were unkind. We were both guilty of that. But I . . . I simply cannot be sure of the reason for his silence. And I need to know."

Sympathy welled inside Roger. Heavy snows and harsh conditions closed the park to visitors in the winter. Even if her brother had been at the hotel on the lake last September, he would have had to leave not many weeks later. He could be anywhere in the country by this time. What did she hope to find?

As if reading his thoughts, she continued, "Grayson

said he'd made friends with people who worked at the hotel. I'm hoping one of them can tell me where he went from there."

Roger had learned last year that the hotel employed about forty people to serve their guests. How many of those employees returned from one season to the next? Could Victoria be fortunate enough to find even one among them who had befriended her brother? To have come so far when her chances of success were that small revealed a great need in her heart. In response, a desire to help her succeed rose inside of him. A desire he didn't welcome.

THE SUN WAS LOWERING in the western sky when Victoria felt the coach slow once again. Was it time for another change of horses? Were they about to make another steep climb? Had another stagecoach lost a wheel?

Roger leaned toward the window. "We're here," he said as he sat back again.

"We are?" Hope swelled within. She'd made it. She'd reached her destination. Perhaps, God willing, she would discover Grayson's whereabouts even today.

The moment the coach came to a complete stop, a porter opened the door, ready to help the passengers to the ground. The young man smiled when he saw Victoria and offered a hand to her. Grateful, she took it, uncertain whether she could have disembarked without the assistance.

While she waited for Roger, she looked at the two-story white wooden structure. It had a restrained Colonial Revival style with a wide porch supported by sturdy columns. Guests sat in the shaded area, taking in the breathtaking views of the shimmering lake and surrounding wilderness.

"If you'll come with me," the porter said.

Roger fell into step behind Victoria as she followed the porter inside.

The lobby wasn't especially large but it felt welcoming with its thick rugs covering the wooden floor and soothing piano music coming from an adjoining room.

A desk clerk in formal attire stood behind the reception counter, smiling as they approached. "Welcome to the Yellowstone Lake Hotel, madam."

"Thank you."

The clerk's gaze slid beyond her shoulder, and she knew he'd spotted Roger, thinking they were together. The idea made her feel strangely warm inside.

"Please," Roger said, "assist Miss Castleton first."

The clerk looked at her again, his expression revealing no embarrassment. "Of course. Castleton, did you say?"

"Yes, Victoria Castleton."

His eyes searched a book on the counter before him. "Yes, Miss Castleton. I have a room reserved for you." He slid a guestbook toward her. "If you will sign here, please."

While she wrote her name in the register, the clerk motioned for a bellman, handed him a key, and told him what room was to be hers. Before she could be led away, she faced Roger. "Thank you again, Mr. Bernhardt. I will never forget your kindness."

"You are ever so welcome, Miss Castleton." He bowed his head briefly. "I'm glad I could be of service to you." He hesitated another moment, then said, "Perhaps you would care to join me for dinner in about an hour."

Her answer came quickly. "I should like that." Only then did she realize how much she'd dreaded an evening alone. Surprising, given how eager she'd been to reach her destination.

"How absolutely splendid." He grinned. "I shall meet you in the parlor by the piano."

With a slight nod of acknowledgment, she turned and followed a bellman—about the same age as Grayson—out of the lobby and along a hallway, almost to the end of the corridor. The bellman unlocked and opened the door before her.

The guest room was modestly sized and minimally furnished with a bed, a washstand, a chair, and a small writing desk near the window that looked out upon the lake, now glittering with late afternoon sunlight. Before she could move deeper into the room, a second bellman entered the room with her trunk and valise and set them on the floor at the foot of the bed.

She retrieved two dimes from her reticule and gave one to each of the bellmen. "Thank you."

They bobbed their heads before retreating into the hallway.

Alone in her room, she wondered if she'd made a mistake accepting Roger's invitation to dine with him. A part of her wished to undress and climb into bed and sleep. But would she sleep yet? Her thoughts and emotions were churning even now.

She looked down at her traveling gown. It was covered with dust as it had been the day before and the day before that. The dresses in her trunk would be cleaner but heavily wrinkled. No, a good shake and a brushing of the gown she wore would have to do for this evening. She would ask to have the dresses in her trunk cleaned and pressed tomorrow. And what did it matter? She didn't need to impress Roger Bernhardt. They had traveled together for the past two days. He'd surely seen her at her worst. As for other guests she might encounter, she didn't need to impress them either. Her only concern was finding her brother. That was all that mattered.

Chapter Five

As a clock in the lobby struck the hour, Victoria entered the hotel parlor. Roger waited for her there, as he'd said he would. She thought it entirely unfair that he looked as fresh now as when they'd started out that morning. Despite her efforts to clean away traces of the days of travel, she felt bedraggled by comparison.

He offered his arm, and they walked together to the dining hall. It was an expansive room, ready for many more guests than what it held at present. Tables throughout were covered with pristine white tablecloths and set with fine china and crystal, as if prepared for a king's banquet. A white-gloved waitstaff took orders and delivered meals. Diners ate, chatted, and looked out the wall of windows at the still waters.

Victoria could scarcely catch her breath as she sank into her chair. Beyond the wide panes of glass, Yellowstone Lake shimmered like a sheet of polished silver, broken here and there by the dark green rise of forested hills. Farther away, the mountains lifted their rugged peaks against an impossibly blue sky. "It really is quite beautiful," she said softly, knowing the words were inadequate.

"Extraordinary."

When she turned from the view, she discovered him watching her instead of the view beyond the windows. Warmth swirled in her belly. Disturbed by it, she took her spectacles from her reticule and settled them on the bridge of her nose. Then she lifted the menu and perused it. Instead of distracting her, the choices felt overwhelming. She set down the menu and rubbed her right temple with her fingertips, eyes now closed.

"Are you all right, Miss Castleton?"

"Yes. No. I . . . I seem to have a headache."

"Not surprising. It's been a long journey. Or it could be caused by the high altitude. That can make some people dreadfully ill." He leaned back in his chair. "Would you like me to order for you?"

The question made her pulse skip and her throat thicken. No one had offered to take care of her in such a long, long while. From the age of sixteen, she had made every decision that had to be made. Concerning herself. Concerning her home. Concerning Grayson before he left Boston. How afraid she'd been that she would make a wrong choice. One that would ruin her brother. And how certain she was she'd done just that.

Realizing Roger waited for an answer, she nodded as she removed her glasses and put them back in their case.

The waiter—a young man in his twenties—arrived. "May I take your order?"

He didn't look anything like Grayson, but he reminded Victoria of her brother, all the same. Surely he was someone Grayson might have befriended. She forgot her headache. "Excuse me."

His gaze slid to her. "Yes, madam?"

"Did you work at this hotel last summer?"

"No, madam. This is my first summer in the park."

Disappointment replaced hope. "Thank you." She lowered her gaze.

"Of course. Sir? Are you ready to order?"

"Yes." Roger cleared his throat. "We'll begin with the deviled eggs with fresh dill and Yellowstone trout chowder." He ran his finger down the menu. "The watercress salad with lemon dressing sounds good. For the main course we'll have the roasted saddle of venison with mashed potatoes and gravy and green beans almondine. And we'll end with the strawberry shortcake."

"Very good, sir." The waiter took the menus and walked away.

"He's only one employee, Miss Castleton." Roger's voice was low and filled with tenderness.

She drew in a breath. "I know."

"You need a hearty meal and a good night's sleep. Tomorrow will look a little brighter."

How could he know what she needed? He was a man. And a man without a care in the world. He traveled in a private coach. He came to the park to do nothing but draw and paint for weeks. True, he said he was without family, but he had friends and he had means to do as he pleased.

"If you like, I will ask about your brother too. Most days I shall be going out beyond the confines of this hotel. I'll talk with the men who take visitors on sightseeing trips and out on the lake. I can ask at the general store and at the stables."

His offer overwhelmed her once again. It wasn't his fault that he enjoyed benefits she did not. And he had been nothing but polite and kind.

He leaned toward her again. "Do you have a photograph of Grayson?"

"I did, but it was lost somewhere on my way west." Tears welled in her eyes. "I don't know how it happened. One morning I simply couldn't find it. It must have fallen from my reticule."

"That is unfortunate. But perhaps, if you describe him to me, I could sketch a picture for you to use when making your inquiries. I was commissioned to paint a few portraits back in England. Those paintings were rather good, I was told. Of course, my subjects were seated before me as I worked, but I will try to capture your description."

"You would do that for me?" she whispered, unshed tears blurring her vision.

THE VULNERABILITY in her question pained Roger. "Of course I will." The responding gratitude in her eyes bothered him even more. And no wonder. He hadn't come to the park to become embroiled in another person's problems. He wasn't here to look for a missing brother, no matter how beloved. Why was he allowing that to happen?

"Mr. Bernhardt, I'm afraid I can't afford to pay you for a portrait."

Her lack of funds was the perfect excuse to withdraw his offer. He could have nodded in agreement and let the matter drop. And yet the words that came out of his mouth were, "I do not require payment, Miss Castleton. It will be my pleasure to help you in this way."

The waiter returned to the table, carrying the platter of appetizers. He set the deviled eggs in the center of the table, nodded, and left. The interruption was brief but long enough for Roger to swallow any other promises he might have made. Instead, he motioned toward the platter. "Please, Miss Castleton. Help yourself."

Light reflecting off the lake cast a glow behind Victoria, and Roger couldn't help thinking how he would paint *her* if he had the chance. Perhaps standing in a field of tall golden grass, the wind tugging at her dark hair. Perhaps with her hair down around her shoulders instead of swept high on her head. Her eyes would be lowered, as they were now. No, it would be a crime not to paint her eyes. They were so expressive. He would have her look at him as he painted.

As if hearing him demand that very thing, she looked up. After a few moments, she asked, "Why do you stare at me that way?" There was a soft tremble in her voice.

He blinked. "I . . . I'm sorry. It's just that I have a

strange feeling I should know you from somewhere." That was the truth, too, but he dare not tell her that he'd also been imagining what it would be like to paint her portrait.

"Know me?"

Shaking his head slowly, he frowned. "It makes no sense, I realize. From our conversations over the past two days, it is clear we've never even been in the same cities. And yet I can't stop thinking I have seen you before."

"I must look like someone you've met."

"Yes, that must be it." He offered a slight incline of his head. "And I promise I will do my best not to stare at you because of it."

He would try. But could he succeed?

Chapter Six

Victoria awakened the following morning, thankful she didn't have to rush to board another coach. She didn't know for certain how many days she would remain at the Lake Hotel, but she'd reserved the room for two weeks. And after that? She didn't know. If she met someone who could tell her about Grayson's time in the park or where he might have gone from there, perhaps she would leave sooner. But what if she learned nothing? What if her trip across the country brought her no answers? What would she do then? Go home and hope to hear from him eventually? And then what? She couldn't remember when she'd ever felt so adrift.

She rose and went to the window where she pushed aside the curtains. The lake appeared like a sheet of glass, sunlight reflecting off its still surface. So unlike the way she felt on the inside. She was a practical person. She liked living her life by a plan. Coming in search of Grayson hadn't been practical, and beyond knowing the park was her destination, there hadn't been much of a plan. She hated the chaos the unknown stirred within. She wanted peace, like the lake at this moment.

"God is in control," her mother used to say.

Victoria tried to believe it. But her life seemed out of control and had felt that way for many, many years. Death and loss. Struggle and strife. That's what she'd known. And after Grayson left Boston, she'd had to face it alone.

Fingertips against the windowpane, she whispered, "Perhaps I shouldn't be here. Will any good come of it?"

Grayson's childhood face appeared in her memory. Smiling. Laughing. Her half-brother, two years her junior, had been such a happy boy. Before the family fortunes took an abrupt turn for the worse, the two of them had run through the Castleton mansion, hiding from maids and tutors as well as their parents. Later, in a much smaller house with only one servant, Grayson had remained much the same while Victoria had become more serious, more afraid of what else might happen to upend their world. Perhaps that was when the true separation between siblings had begun. Even before more happened. And more *had* happened.

Taking care of Grayson had filled Victoria's days after typhoid fever took their mother and his father to the grave. Victoria's primary goal in the beginning had been to make certain Grayson finished his schooling. Her fourteen-year-old brother had insisted he could get work to help support them, but her wishes had prevailed. At first anyway. But by the time her brother turned seventeen, he'd stopped listening to her. He'd taken a job on the docks, and in his free time, he'd sketched the people and the world around him.

She turned from the window and the serene lake beyond, her troubled thoughts continuing to churn.

It had been the small inheritance from an uncle she'd never known—Lester Castleton, the estranged brother of her father—that had first improved and then torn apart her life. The legacy hadn't made Victoria and Grayson rich by any means, but it had removed her ever-present fear of losing their small home or going without the basics of a genteel life. It had also set Grayson free to do as he willed.

"You'll be all right without me," he shouted in her memory. "You don't need the money I earn on the docks. Vicky, if I don't go now, I'll never go. I'll never get away to see what else I can do with my life."

"You can explore other means of making a living here in Boston," she'd responded.

"It isn't about that. I'll go mad if I stay here. You don't understand. You'll never understand." He'd stormed out of the house, slamming the door behind him.

Victoria sank onto the nearby chair, her heart racing as fast now as it had at the time of the argument. And Grayson had been right. She still didn't understand, not even after the passage of more than two years. But if she could find him, she would tell him she was sorry for not trying harder, for not listening better.

"Please, God. Let me find him. Let me tell him."

WITH ONE KNEE bent so he could rest the sketchpad on his thigh, Roger leaned his back against a fallen tree. The sound of lake water lapping the shore joined with the rustle of forest creatures moving through underbrush and of birds fluttering from branch to branch.

To his left, perhaps thirty yards from where he sat, a doe and two fawns walked out of the trees to the water's edge. If he moved, the doe and her offspring would bound back into the safety of the forest. And so he held his hand steady, resisting the urge to draw, instead trying to memorize the way the deer stood, the way they moved on their delicate legs, the caramel color of their coats, the alertness in the mother's large eyes. But even his practiced stillness wasn't enough to hide him for long from the beautiful creatures. The doe saw him, froze for a moment, then ran to safety, the fawns following after her.

He smiled. One year ago, he had found this place about a thirty minute walk from the Lake Hotel. That morning, he'd sat with his back against this same log and sketched waterfowl gliding on the lake as the sun rose above the mountains in the east. It felt good to be back. Like coming home. But this time, he'd come for a longer stay.

Profound gratitude to God welled within. He might not be as verbal about his faith as some he knew, but his silence didn't lessen his belief in the goodness of the Lord and how thankful he was for it. "All this You made," he whispered, his gaze taking in the beauty surrounding him. "All this You own."

In the quietude surrounding him, he mused upon all

that had happened to him in the past year and a half. Roger Bernhardt, who had never in his life traveled farther from London than Lincolnshire, who had never even crossed the English Channel, had said yes to his friend's invitation to go to America. When he agreed to the trip, Roger hadn't imagined all he would find in this country or how his life would change because of it. He certainly hadn't known he would decide to stay for good. That decision still surprised him, as it had others. Even Amanda, who herself had chosen to remain—although her decision had been made when she lost her heart to an American—hadn't believed it when he'd told her.

A ground squirrel hopped onto the opposite end of the log, drawing his attention. As the small creature rose on its hind legs, its front legs crossed over its chest, Roger began to sketch. Something about the squirrel made him grin as he drew it, doing his best to show with a pencil its grayish back and rump with its fine white spots. The ground squirrel sniffed the air. Perhaps it realized the human had no food with him and cared about nothing but his artwork. Roger would have sworn he saw a look of disdain on the rodent's tiny face before it jumped off the log and scurried away.

He laughed. "I'm hungry too, little guy." He rose from the ground, put his few supplies into a canvas bag, and began the walk back to the hotel.

***

VICTORIA WAS SEATED on the porch when Roger approached, sketchpad in hand. In a way, she was surprised that he'd remembered to meet her there. Even more so that he was right on time. Her brother had often forgotten his promises and was even more apt to be tardy.

"Good morning." He sat in a nearby chair.

As she smiled in response, she realized she was glad to see him—and not only because of his promise to draw her brother. "Good morning."

"Have you done any exploring?" he asked.

"No. But I've talked to a few of the employees about Grayson."

"Any luck?"

She shook her head.

"I'm sorry. But maybe we can help with that." He settled the pad of paper on his lap and held his pencil between the fingers of his right hand, ready to begin.

The discouragement of earlier that morning tried to raise its ugly head, but Victoria pushed it back.

"Let me begin with a few questions about Grayson. Does he look a lot like you?"

She frowned in thought. "Not a great deal. We both have our mother's nose. Or so she always told us. My hair is a much darker brown than his. I always thought his was kissed by the sun."

A smile tugged at his mouth as he started to sketch. "How about the shape of his face?"

"I think much the same as mine." This was more difficult than she'd anticipated. She scarcely could remember the shape of her own face, let alone her brother's. "His chin is more square than mine. Mine's more pointed."

Roger didn't look at her when he said, "You have a lovely chin, Miss Castleton."

Her stomach fluttered. A silly reaction because she was convinced his words meant nothing. He may not have realized he even said them. He probably paid similar compliments to anyone as he drew them. Words to put them at ease. Not that he was drawing her. He was attempting to sketch a likeness of Grayson.

Roger asked more questions, and his pencil never stopped moving. Was Grayson's hair worn long or short? Did it part on the side or in the center? Were his eyes round or oval? Were his brows thick or thin? Did those brows arch in the center or toward the end? Was his neck long? Were his shoulders narrow or broad? Did he have a beard or was he clean shaven? As the drawing took shape, she offered corrections, although trying to explain what she meant wasn't easy. But Roger hardly seemed to notice that she struggled with her descriptions. He remained calm and focused.

"And now?" He turned the sketch for her to see.

Although she'd looked at it several times during the process, the end result still surprised her. "That's him. That's Grayson. Very close, at least." She reached out to touch the likeness. "It's much like the photograph I had of him. Only larger, of course."

"Perfect." He carefully removed the paper from the sketchpad and offered it to her. "I hope it makes a difference."

Tears rose suddenly in her eyes. "You are inordinately kind, Mr. Bernhardt. I shall never forget."

Chapter Seven

The log chapel was set back from the road leading to the hotel. Roger heard voices raised in song as he approached the church building and realized he was late for the morning service. He hurried inside, stepping into the back pew as the hymn came to a close.

"Welcome," the man behind the lectern said in a deep voice. "I'm Reverend Robertson. Welcome to the Chapel by the Lake."

Roger's gaze moved over the congregation in the rows before him. About twenty people in all. Some undoubtedly were employees of the Lake Hotel. Others were tourists. The latter stood out based on their attire alone. Particularly women who wore tight corsets beneath gowns of expensive fabric with enormous puffed sleeves.

He noticed Victoria Castleton then, a few pews in front of him and to the far right. Her serge gown, cobalt blue in color, was much more practical for this wilderness location. His own knowledge of the type of fabric brought a rueful smile to his lips. A draper's son apparently never forgot such details.

The pastor preached from the book of Ezekiel, a sermon that challenged his listeners to consume the word of the Lord—to eat the scroll, as God told the prophet—and be filled with it in their daily lives.

After the service, Roger paused outside the church to stare at the unblemished sky. Not a bird. Not a cloud.

"It's beautiful," came Victoria's voice behind him.

He turned to face her.

"Do you wish to paint everything you see?" A whisper of a smile tipped the corners of her mouth.

He chuckled. "Not everything." He searched his mind for an example, then continued with a serious expression, "I do not recall feeling an urge to paint a privy."

She laughed, and by her expression, he surmised her reaction had surprised even her. And for some reason, he felt inordinately pleased with himself that he'd been able to bring her that moment of amusement.

In an unspoken agreement, they turned toward the hotel and started to walk.

"Have you done a lot of painting since I saw you last, Mr. Bernhardt?"

"I spent the past couple of days along the river north of here. There's a spot where buffalo and elk and other wildlife come to water, and another place that gave me a great view of an eagle's nest." He glanced at her. "And you? Have you had any success?"

No smile curved her mouth now. "Not really. I confirmed that Grayson was a guest at the hotel in

September of last year. And yesterday I spoke to a young woman who remembers him. One of the maids. But she said she never spoke to him. She simply saw him sketching the lake. But she promised to introduce me to one of the bellmen whom she believes knew Grayson well. Perhaps I'll meet him this afternoon."

"That sounds hopeful."

"I want to believe it will make a difference. That someone will be able to tell me where he went after his stay here. But I fear I'm on a fool's errand." She made a sweeping motion with her arm. "Look where we are. This vast wilderness that surrounds us. It goes on forever, well beyond the boundaries of the park. Grayson could have gone anywhere after his stay at this hotel. Anywhere at all."

Roger wished he could say something to encourage her. But what? She was right. Her brother could be anywhere. He'd had that same thought himself.

There was another question that had plagued him for the past few days. It concerned the drawing he'd made of her brother. Something nagged at Roger, the feeling that he should know the young man his own hand had drawn. He'd felt the same way about Victoria when he'd first seen her. Now her brother too. But he hadn't met Victoria before nor had he met any man named Grayson. It wasn't a common name. Surely he would have remembered someone who wore it.

"Have I said something amiss, Mr. Bernhardt."

He blinked. "Sorry?"

"You were frowning, as if I'd said something to upset you."

He stopped walking, causing her to do the same. "You didn't upset me, Miss Castleton, but I confess something does trouble me. It has to do with your brother. I can't shake the feeling that I have seen him before."

"You think you saw him?"

"Yes. And that I've seen you as well."

She took a half step back from him, perhaps fearing he'd lost his senses. He couldn't blame her for that. Sometimes he wondered the same.

Roger motioned toward the porch of the hotel. "Would you sit with me and allow me to explain?"

She nodded.

After they settled onto a couple of chairs, Roger told Victoria about the day he'd seen her from across the street, outside the hotel in Gardiner, how her face had seemed familiar to him and that the feeling hadn't gone away during their two-day journey into the park. "I had the same feeling when I finished the sketch of your brother," he added. "As I said already, I simply cannot shake it. He looks very familiar to me. And I daresay not because you share a few similar features or merely because I did the sketch."

Victoria's hands clenched in her lap, confusion written on her face. "As we've discussed before, I have never been outside of Boston until I made this trip west. You could not possibly have seen me. But it's possible you met Grayson. Were you in Yellowstone last fall?"

"No. In mid-summer."

She shook her head. "Then you could not have met up with him in the park. He arrived from Colorado at the end of August. Did you spend any time in that state?"

"Again, no. My friends and I came straight from New York City to Idaho in the spring of last year."

"Then I can only conclude once again that you are mistaken about recognizing us, Mr. Bernhardt. My brother and I must look like someone else you've met on your travels."

She glanced away from him, and her crestfallen expression made him wish he'd never brought it up.

***

VICTORIA LOOKED out at the lake as she pushed down her disappointment. It would have been a miracle if Grayson had crossed paths with Roger, and miracles were in short supply in her experience.

"Miss Castleton?"

She turned to see Grace Short—the maid she'd spoken with the previous day—walking toward her, a uniformed bellman at her side. Hope sprang to life for the second time that morning.

"Miss Castleton, this is Bernard Fields. He worked at the hotel last summer and remembers your brother."

Victoria's pulse quickened as her gaze shot to the bellman. "You knew Grayson?"

"Yes, miss. I did. When I wasn't on duty, we hiked around the lake together. Grayson and I became good friends."

She rose from the chair. "In his last letter to me, he said he would leave the park because winter weather approached. Do you know where he went when he left the hotel?"

"Sorry. He didn't say and I didn't think to ask. All I know is, he took the stage back to Gardiner with other park visitors. We, the employees, were all getting ready to head to our own homes for the winter so it didn't seem important to ask about his own destination."

Victoria regained her seat as a wave of dismay washed over her.

Bernard cleared his throat. "If I may, Miss Castleton."

She looked up.

"Grayson left behind all his art supplies and the drawings and a few paintings that he did while he was in the park. He was plenty discouraged by then. He said he didn't have enough talent as an artist and was going to stop trying. I don't know much about art, but I thought he was good. Anyway, I stored all those belongings in a box in case he came back for them."

Tears welled in her eyes. "That was kind of you."

"Since he never came back, I guess it all belongs to you by rights. I can bring the box to your guest room if you'd like."

"I would like that. Thank you."

Bernard offered a nod of his head and Grace gave a small curtsey. Then both walked away.

After a lengthy silence in their wake, Roger said, "Perhaps you'll find a clue in the things Grayson left behind."

She blinked away the tears. "I'm afraid of what I might find. Or maybe I'm afraid I'll find nothing at all."

She took a deep breath and let it out slowly. Then she straightened her back and leveled her shoulders, at the same time lifting her chin in a show of strength. A strength she didn't feel.

"If I can be of any further assistance." Roger rose from the chair.

"You have done so much already."

He acknowledged her words with a bob of his head before departing.

Stillness swirled around her, accompanied by a fear that she would forever be alone. Not just that she wouldn't find her brother but that she wouldn't have anyone else in her life from now until the day she died. The feelings were much too close to self-pity for comfort. She despised self-pity. She was stronger than that. She'd had to be, even as a child.

Swallowing the thickness in her throat, she stood and went to her room to await Bernard.

Chapter Eight

A few hours later, Victoria sat on the floor in her room, papers and canvases scattered around her. She'd paid little heed to the art supplies in the box Bernard delivered a short while before. Those things could tell her nothing. They were exactly the same now as they'd been in Boston. But the sketches and water-color paintings. She hoped these might hold a clue. Only what? She needed to know where he was now. Not what he'd seen while he was at the hotel.

The paintings were of the wilderness, the moun-tains, the wildlife.

"He said he didn't have enough talent as an artist and was going to stop trying."

As the bellman's words replayed in her memory, she studied a watercolor of the lake at sunset. She thought it pretty, the colors delicate, but she was no judge. Knowing it was Grayson's might influence her opinion. Perhaps Roger Bernhardt could look at it and say what he thought.

"What difference would that make?" she whispered as she set the picture aside.

She picked up three pencil sketches. They were all of the same woman, one of her standing by the lake, another of her seated on a fallen tree in the forest, and in the last, she was leaning on a balcony railing, her head thrown back in laughter. Even Victoria could see the difference in ability between these drawings and the one Roger had made of Grayson. Roger was definitely more skilled as an artist. She touched the drawing of the laughing woman with a fingertip. "You liked her. Didn't you?" Pulse quickening, she pushed up from the floor and headed out of her room, the three sketches in hand.

The older gentleman who worked the front desk most days was standing behind the counter when she entered the lobby. He grinned and greeted her by name.

"Mr. Matthews," she said as she drew close. "I found some drawings my brother did." She didn't need to explain. She had talked with the man at length about Grayson a couple of days before. "Do you happen to recognize her?" She placed the papers on the counter before him.

The desk clerk frowned in concentration as he looked from one drawing to the next. "You know, I think I do recall her face. She was a guest during the time your brother was with us. Don't recollect her name right off, but maybe if I looked at the register from last year. Seems like she was here with a brother or a cousin. Let me have a look-see. I might be able to come up with her name."

She beamed at the man. "Thank you, Mr.

Matthews." She gathered the three drawings and pressed them against her chest.

"Check back with me before you go in to supper. I should have time to check by then."

"I shall do that." She turned away, her heart feeling lighter than it had in months. Perhaps in years.

She went outside, too excited to return to her room just yet. It wasn't until she saw Roger at the far end of the porch, looking toward the lake, that she realized she'd hoped to find him there. "Mr. Bernhardt?"

He turned, his expression composed. "You found something?" he asked as she approached.

"I think so. Yes." When she reached him, she held out the drawings. "It may be nothing, but I can't help thinking this woman could be a clue."

Roger cocked an eyebrow before taking the papers from her. He studied each one of them carefully. Once. Then again.

Anxiety tightened her chest.

He looked up. "Your brother is not without talent, Miss Castleton."

"I wish he could hear you say so."

"What was it you saw in these?"

"That he . . . that he liked his subject. This woman was more than just a person to draw. There are feelings there. Perhaps he loved her?" She said the last as a question, beginning to doubt herself.

But Roger's smile returned. "I believe you are right." He perused each of the drawings once again. "Yes, I see it too. There is affection in the pencil strokes. The artist captured more than her pretty appearance. He sought to portray her heart as well."

A longing swirled inside Victoria at his words. A desire to have a man look at her and feel about her what Grayson seemed to have felt for the young woman in the drawing.

Roger said, "We should ask if anyone remembers her."

She felt a little thrill over the word "we." She shouldn't, of course. This was her quest. How many times could she expect Roger Bernhardt to come to her aid? She tamped down the emotion as she answered, "I already asked at the front desk. Mr. Matthews recognized her and said he would check the register from last autumn to see if he can discover her name."

"Splendid!" Roger's smile chased away the shadows on the porch.

"Yes. It is splendid, isn't it?"

He kept smiling, and she felt captured by his blue eyes. The way he looked at her . . . What did he see?

His smile fell away. "Miss Castleton." He paused, as if unsure what he wanted to say. "Would you . . . would you care to take a walk with me along the lake? I ate a rather large lunch, and I could use a stretch of the legs." He motioned with his hand. "The day is rather fine."

Why did she suddenly find it difficult to breathe?

"I would appreciate your company," he added.

Pulse fluttering in her chest, she nodded. "I would enjoy a walk, Mr. Bernhardt. Let me return these drawings to my room and get my hat. I won't be long."

ROGER WONDERED over his invitation for Victoria to join him on a walk. Why had he done it? He spent a great deal of his time alone and never minded it. In fact, he preferred solitude. Or, at least, he'd always thought so.

As he waited for her, he turned to gaze over the lake again. The expanse of water mirrored the sky. This morning, there'd been a gentle blush of pink and gold dancing across the surface of the lake, as soft as a watercolor wash. Now, at midday, the color of the water had deepened to sapphire.

He wasn't happy with his most recent attempts to capture the lake on canvas. Perhaps it eluded him because the lake was always changing. The same water didn't remain in one place. It moved. It ebbed and flowed. The river fed into the lake at one end and the river carried the water out at the other end. Water that moved was living. It nurtured life. Water that was trapped became stagnant. He was reminded that God offered living water to His children, and desire tugged at his heart, a desire to reveal such a truth through one of his paintings. Was that possible?

He turned at the sound of footsteps behind him. Victoria was there, still wearing the blue serge gown she'd worn to church that morning, but now sporting a broad-brimmed straw hat.

"Ready?" He offered his elbow.

She slipped her fingers into the crook of his arm. "Yes."

Together they followed a path to the shoreline. Once

there, she stopped, let go of his arm, and turned her face to the sun, one hand on the crown of her hat lest the lake breezes take it from her, and the look of her captured him completely. The length and bend of her throat. The long, loose strands of dark hair that curled against her back. The delicate color in the apple of her cheeks.

Zounds! He would like to paint her like that. She was beyond beautiful with the water behind her and towering pines, standing like silent sentinels off to one side of the frame he imagined.

"I have long enjoyed the seashore." She straightened, her gaze turned upon the lake. "At the ocean I feel the surge and a power that is almost frightening. But this is serene. It leaves me feeling . . . peaceful. Don't you find it so?"

He answered in the affirmative while mentally he selected paints that would bring out the golden shade of her straw hat and the blue of her gown that brightened with the lake behind her.

She glanced in his direction and seemed to realize he'd been staring at her for a long while. The rosy tint in her cheeks turned to a flush of embarrassment.

Sorry the vision he'd had of her was broken, he turned and began to stroll along the shore, his hands clasped behind his back. He kept his pace slow and leisurely, allowing her time to gather herself and catch up with him. Neither spoke for a long while.

As they rounded a bend, Roger put out an arm to indicate they should stop. Then he pointed.

Ahead of them, a doe and fawn stepped into the

shallows of the lake, their tawny coats a warm contrast against the cool hues of water and stone. Each step caused a ripple that distorted their reflections, a fleeting impression beneath the deer, like an unfinished brushstroke.

Roger heard Victoria's sigh of delight. So did the doe, and she quickly led her fawn back into the safety of the forest.

"They're such graceful animals," she whispered.

"Indeed. But they take flight at the slightest sound or motion. It isn't easy to sketch one of them up close. Believe me. I've tried."

She turned to face him. "Mr. Bernhardt, would it be terribly presumptuous of me to ask to see some of your paintings?"

"Not at all, Miss Castleton. I believe I would rather like getting your opinion of my art."

A smile bowed the corners of her mouth, and he found himself wishing to explore those lips. Not with a paintbrush on canvas but with his own lips.

Dash it all! He'd better get control of himself. He hadn't come to America to become involved with a woman. Not this woman. Not any woman. He wasn't like Sebastian and Amanda, looking for adventure but delighted when they found romance as well.

"Perhaps we should make our way back to the hotel," Victoria said softly. "It looks as if it might storm."

Shaking off his troublesome thoughts, he turned his head, surprised to find dark clouds building in the western sky. "You're right. We had better start back."

They'd covered about half of the distance to the hotel when the wind picked up. No longer a gentle breeze meant to cool the warmth of July, it whipped Victoria's skirts around her ankles and tried to tear away her pretty straw hat.

Seeing the clouds—their bellies swollen with rain—approach with surprising speed, Roger reached out and cupped Victoria's elbow. "We'd best hurry or we'll be wet through."

Leaning into the wind, they broke into a jog and arrived at the porch of the hotel as the first raindrops began to fall.

"We made it," she said, laughter in her voice.

The storm descended with fury. The once-still waters of the lake churned with white-capped waves. The wind howled through the pines, their branches looking like desperate arms reaching out against the storm's wrath. Sheets of rain lashed the sides of the hotel and reached beneath one end of the porch to dampen the skirts and pant legs of the intrepid souls who remained outdoors. Lightning fractured the sky, its jagged brilliance illuminating the roiling clouds. A crack of thunder followed a heartbeat after. Victoria jumped at the sound, then seemed transfixed as the thunder rolled across the lake, like a drumbeat of the heavens.

But it was Victoria who captured Roger's attention. He watched as she pulled the straw hat from her head, perhaps tired of trying to keep it in place. The wind pulled more of her hair free from pins and ribbon, making her look almost as wild as the storm itself.

Oh, to paint her like this. It would be even better

than when they'd stood near the lake, her face turned toward the sun. And he realized, as the storm raged on, that he'd begun to feel something in his heart for Victoria unlike anything he'd felt for a woman before. The discovery both intrigued and alarmed him.

Chapter Nine

Roger stood at the edge of the deep river gorge, his gaze tracing the wild beauty before him. For the past few days, he'd positioned himself at different viewpoints above the Grand Canyon of the Yellowstone, attempting to replicate its beauty on canvas. Yesterday, he'd finally come close, although he knew he could never do this view complete justice.

The walls of the canyon blazed with color—ochre, gold, russet, and deep sienna. Morning sunlight brushed the rocks while shadows pooled in crevices, lending depth and mystery to God's creation. Far below him, the river surged, a ribbon of turquoise and frothy white. The roar of the water came to him in an endless symphony of power. Mist from the waterfall rose and scattered into a thousand tiny rainbows.

"Are you ready, Roger?"

He turned to face Teddy Hendrick, the guide who'd brought him from the hotel on Monday and stayed to set up camp and cook meals for him. Four days later,

Roger had gained a new friend, and with all of his supplies and completed paintings safely packed once again, the two of them were about to begin the trip back to the hotel. And he was eager to return. Because as much as he'd loved these days of painting by the canyon, his thoughts had often been set on a dark-haired woman, standing by the lake, her head tilted back, her face turned toward the sun. Or the same young woman with the wind tugging at her hair, her eyes wide at the flash of lightning and the sound of thunder.

"I'm ready," he answered, taking one last glance at the canyon wall opposite him before walking away.

"Never gets old, that view."

Roger stepped up onto the wagon seat. "I do not believe it ever would. Even if I were to see it every day for the rest of my life."

"You're a good artist, you know." Teddy joined him on the wagon seat and took up the reins. "Not that I know much about such things. But plenty of folks come to the park to try to paint what they see. It's not many who come close the way you do."

"Thank you, Teddy. It is kind of you to say so."

"Not kind." The guide clucked to the horses, slapping the reins against their rumps. "Just the truth."

They set off on a rough trail that would take them to the main road, a long day of travel before them.

MR. MATTHEWS HADN'T BEEN able to give Victoria the name of the young woman in Grayson's sketches, and so she'd spent the rest of the week that followed showing her brother's likeness and one of the unnamed woman to every bellman, maid, clerk, waiter, waitress, chef, and kitchen worker employed by the hotel. She'd spoken to the hotel manager and the grooms in the stables. She'd walked to the mercantile that served park employees and guests. There, she'd talked to the proprietors and customers. A few people had recognized Grayson's face, but no one knew him well or knew where he'd gone from Yellowstone. By Friday she feared she'd reached a dead end, and her heart ached because of it.

Loathe though she was to admit it, her sadness was exacerbated by Roger Bernhardt's absence. On the day after the big storm, a guide had taken him north to the Grand Canyon of the Yellowstone, and he hadn't said when he would return. It troubled her that he hadn't felt it important to tell her. And it troubled her more how much she missed him. How she looked for him in the dining hall or on the hotel porch, even when she knew he wouldn't be there. How she wished she could tell him about the people she'd talked with, about her disappointment and discouragement.

VICTORIA WAS RETURNING from an early evening stroll by the lake when she saw Roger stepping down from a wagon, his clothing rumpled, as if he'd lived in the same shirt and trousers the entire time he'd been away. He looked both tired and pleased. The driver lowered the gate on the back of the wagon, and the two men began to unload the crates that protected his finished artwork.

When he saw her approach, a grin split his face. "Miss Castleton, it's grand to see you again."

"And you, Mr. Bernhardt. Was it a successful excursion?"

"I believe so. I do believe so."

"I hope you'll allow me to see some of your paintings. I am not likely to visit the Grand Canyon of the Yellowstone before I depart."

His expression sobered. "You're leaving?"

"Not yet. But soon. There is nothing more to keep me here. I have failed to learn anything of my brother's possible whereabouts."

"I'm sorry to hear it."

Her throat thickened with emotion as she nodded, unable to speak. But what more was there to say? She'd failed to find Grayson, and it was time to go home.

The rattle of harness and clatter of horses' hooves drew her attention toward the road. It was the stagecoach from Gardiner. She recognized the driver even before he drew the teams of horses to a halt behind Roger's hired wagon. In short order, the passengers spilled out of the interior. Two couples, one older and one younger, all of them finely attired.

"Thank heaven we are here!" the older woman exclaimed. "I could not bear another hour in that horrid contraption. They should lay train tracks into the park so visitors can travel to the lake in comfort. Why haven't they done so?"

"Mother, please," the younger woman chided.

The sound of wood splintering pulled Victoria around. One of Roger's crates had been dropped from the back of the wagon and the top of the crate knocked free, exposing the paintings inside.

The driver swore beneath his breath. "Sorry, Roger. Hope nothing's damaged."

"Aside from the crate—" Roger squatted to take a better look. "—doesn't appear anything was harmed."

"My word!" Drawn by the commotion, the older woman from the stagecoach walked closer. "Howard, come and see this painting. It is absolutely marvelous. You, sir, did you paint that?"

Roger stood. "I am the artist, madam. Yes."

"Extraordinary. We were at the Grand Canyon of the Yellowstone for a number of days. I never thought to see an oil painting that captured the vibrant colors of the canyon so completely." She pulled a card from her reticule and held it out to Roger. "I am Mrs. Howard Kennedy, and I would very much like to buy that painting if it is for sale." She leaned forward to peer into the box. "Perhaps you would care to show us some of your other works of art as well?"

The older man—Howard, Victoria presumed—arrived to stand beside the woman. "You are correct, Susannah. It is very fine. But could we resume this discussion at another time? I want to get settled into our rooms, and I am hungry and in need of a good meal."

"Of course. Of course." Susannah Kennedy looked at Roger again. "Perhaps we could arrange a time to meet tomorrow. Are you staying at the hotel?"

"I am."

"And may I have your name?"

"I apologize." He inclined his head. "Roger Bernhardt, at your service. A pleasure to make your acquaintance, Mrs. Kennedy."

"Leave word for me at the front desk, if you would. Let me know when you will be available, and we shall talk more." She slipped her hand into the crook of her husband's arm, and they and the younger couple proceeded up the walkway to the entrance of the hotel.

On a breath, Roger said, "That was rather jolly."

Wordlessly, Victoria moved so that she had a better view of the exposed painting. Susannah Kennedy was correct. It was extraordinary. "Will you sell it to her?"

"I suppose it depends upon what she offers."

If Victoria had the option, she would buy the painting before the other woman could. But she didn't have that option. Her finances were not unlimited, and she had wasted too much of what she possessed on this futile trip.

The driver leaned over and drew the lid of the crate back into place. "I'll get this inside for you."

"Thank you, Teddy. I'll be right behind." Roger met Victoria's gaze. "Perhaps we could talk more at dinner?"

Her pulse quickened. "I should like that, Mr. Bernhardt."

He named the time to meet in the hotel parlor, then lifted another crate and went into the hotel.

Feeling light of heart, she followed moments later.

Chapter Ten

The last time Victoria dined with Roger, they'd just arrived after the journey down from Gardiner. She'd scarcely known him then. But that no longer felt true. Odd, since she still hadn't spent a great deal of time in his company over the past nine days.

Tonight she wore her favorite gown, a dress of gold with brown accents. A comb decorated with peach sapphires—one that had belonged to her mother— adorned her hair, and a solitaire necklace with a matching peach sapphire rested in the cleft of her collarbone.

The intense look in Roger's eyes as she entered the hotel parlor told her more about her appearance than the mirror in the guest room. No one had ever called her beautiful. Not her mother. Not her stepfather. Not her brother. But at this moment, beneath Roger's gaze, she almost believed she might be. She moved toward him with a mixture of exhilaration and uncertainty.

"Good evening." He reached for her gloved hand

and raised it to kiss the air just above her fingers. As he straightened, he added, "May I say, you look particularly lovely tonight."

She warmed beneath his compliment. "Thank you, sir." She could have said that he looked particularly lovely as well in his well-cut suit coat and vest.

She took his proffered arm, and together they made their way into the dining hall. Nearly every table in the restaurant was taken, and the sound of many conversations filled the air. Waiters darted to and from the kitchen, carrying trays either laden with food or holding empty plates and bowls.

"Good evening," the maître d' said in welcome. Then he led them to a table for four and pulled out a chair for Victoria. "Enjoy your dinner." He placed a menu in front of each of them before walking away.

Roger looked around the restaurant. "I heard the Wylie Camping Company arrived at the lake this afternoon. Explains why the restaurant is so busy."

"Camping company?"

"Yes, Wylie's has permanent campsites set up around the park. Mammoth Hot Springs, Old Faithful, Canyon, the Norris Geyser Basin, and one here on the lake. The accommodations are surprisingly good. Large canvas tents with wooden floors, stoves for warmth, and real beds. Guests are taken from one site to the next in horse-drawn wagons. I think there are longer tours but the six-day tour seems to be the most popular." He cocked an eyebrow. "Maybe you should try it before you leave the park. You've seen nothing but the lake. Why come all this way and not experience it for yourself?"

Hope warred with practicality. "I wish I could." Practicality won. She needed to remain mindful of the funds that remained in her bank account and how quickly it could drain away. "But I can't."

Disappointment showed on his face. "I am sorry to hear it." With that, he lowered his gaze to the menu.

He was correct, of course. It was a shame to come all this way and not see more of the park. But she had no desire to spend the days in the company of strangers, moving from site to site and sleeping in tents. It might be different if Roger Bernhardt also joined the tour.

Her pulse quickened at the thought. Merciful heavens! Had she lost all touch with reality? Surely it was her brother whom she would want with her. Not the man seated opposite her.

The waiter came and took their orders. Victoria settled on a mixed green salad with a lemon vinaigrette, buttered new potatoes with chives, and the grilled trout. Roger chose the pickled radishes and cucumbers, a bowl of cold cucumber soup, and the roast chicken with asparagus tips.

By the time the waiter left their table, Victoria's pulse had calmed and her feet were once again firmly planted on the ground. After removing her reading spectacles, she glanced across the table, ready to steer the conversation to something other than her upcoming departure, but Roger was suddenly on his feet, grinning widely.

"By heaven!" He lifted a hand, acknowledging someone behind her.

She twisted to look over her shoulder and watched

as a man and a woman wound their way through the tables without waiting for the maître d' to escort them. The beautiful woman—younger than Victoria by a few years, she guessed—was simply dressed in riding boots, a dark brown split skirt that reached her shins, and a rosy-brown blouse. The man with her was ruggedly handsome, his attire well-suited to the wilderness of the park more than this restaurant.

"Roger!" the woman exclaimed as they drew close. "Oh, it is so terribly good to see you." She almost threw herself at him, hugging him close, her cheek pressed against his chest.

Victoria felt a sting of something she didn't care to name.

Roger kissed the woman's forehead before she pulled back from him. "Look at you, Amanda. You have blossomed in your new life." His gaze moved to the man behind her. "Isaiah, it is good to see you again." He held out his hand and they shook. "Join us, please."

The woman, Amanda, turned her gaze on Victoria, curiosity sparking in her dark eyes.

Roger lightly touched Victoria's shoulder. "Miss Castleton, may I introduce my dear friends, Mr. and Mrs. Coltrane. Amanda and I traveled together with her brother from England. Amanda, Isaiah, this is Miss Victoria Castleton. We met on our journey into the park."

Victoria's feelings altered after the introduction. Mr. and *Mrs.* Coltrane. All of a sudden, she was inclined to like them both very much.

As Amanda's gaze swept over the busy restaurant,

she settled onto the chair at Victoria's left while her husband took the chair across from her. "We ate breakfast here a few days after we first met." She looked across the table at Isaiah. "Do you remember?"

"Of course I remember." There was tenderness in both his eyes and his voice.

Victoria felt as if she were intruding on a private moment. Silly, given the number of people crowded into the dining hall.

The waiter returned. "Will you be ordering dinner as well?" he asked Isaiah.

"We will."

Menus were set before the newcomers. "I'll give you a few moments to decide."

"It will be nice to have something to eat besides jerky and hardtack." Amanda lifted the menu to peruse it.

Victoria sent a questioning glance in Roger's direction.

"This is the couple I told you about on our way into the park. They work as game scouts in Yellowstone. Always on the lookout for poachers to arrest and take to the authorities."

"Isaiah is the game scout." Amanda laughed as she shook her head. "I simply ride along. In fact, I doubt they would hire me for such work, no matter how much my skills have improved. But I have learned a great deal this summer. Haven't I, darling?"

"You have, indeed," Isaiah responded. You have, indeed."

THROUGHOUT DINNER, Roger plied Isaiah and Amanda with questions about their home in Montana and their escapades in the park as they tracked and captured poachers. He hadn't realized until now how much he'd missed his friends' presence at Eden's Gate. Especially Amanda's. She livened up any gathering with her cheerful demeanor and delightful conversation.

He noticed Victoria's changing expressions as she listened. Surprise. Disbelief. Consternation. Astonishment. Bafflement. And every alteration made him want to draw her face exactly that way.

They were lingering over dessert and coffee when Amanda turned her attention to Victoria. "We have been terribly rude, have we not? All we have done is talk about ourselves. Please. What about you, Miss Castleton? Are you traveling alone? When I came to the park last year, I was with one of the camping companies, but I didn't continue on with them. That is another story. Won't you be so good as to tell us more about yourself?"

"There isn't much to say." A hint of color rose in Victoria's cheeks.

Amanda laughed again, as she had so often during the meal. "Oh, I doubt that is true. Everyone has a story."

This was not the first time Roger had seen Amanda display her charm and expertise as a hostess, drawing someone into a conversation, making them feel connected and welcome. Many a dinner party at Hooke Manor had been brightened because of her skills.

Little by little, Victoria opened up, sharing more

about her family and especially her brother who—much like Roger himself—had come west to sketch and paint the beauties and wonders of Yellowstone.

Partway through one of her answers, he learned something he hadn't heard before. "Wait. Miss Castleton, did you say Grayson is your *half*-brother? That his father was not your father."

"That's correct."

"Do you share the same last name?"

"No. We don't."

He leaned slightly forward. "I don't believe you told me that before."

"I've spoken to so many people since coming to the park." She shook her head slowly. "I've said his name so often, I didn't realize I hadn't said it to you."

"I've asked around about him. To the different guides. At the general store. But it seems I've been giving the wrong name. I've been asking about Grayson Castleton."

"I'm sorry. I didn't realize. I should have made that clear. His name is Townsend. Grayson Townsend."

"Townsend," Roger echoed softly. The name stirred something in his memory. Was it that name or something else? He remembered Victoria standing outside the hotel in Gardiner, making him wonder if he should know her. He thought of Grayson's image as it came to life in his pencil sketch, somehow familiar but not. "Townsend," he said again, louder this time as the memory came together, like the final brushstroke on a canvas that turns a mixture of colors into a perfect work of art. The man in the sketch had been clean shaven with close-cropped hair. The man he remembered had a beard and hair that brushed his collar. But it was the same man. "Brian Townsend."

Victoria's eyes widened. "Yes. Brian Grayson Townsend. But how did you know? He's always gone by Grayson because his father was also named Brian."

"Miss Castleton, that is no longer true. I've met him. Only once and briefly. It was months ago. He called himself Brian Townsend. Not Grayson." He looked from her to the others, then back again. "I know where he is. Or at least where he was in the spring."

A long silence gripped the table. Even the voices throughout the restaurant seemed to fall away.

Finally, she whispered, "You've met Grayson? But why didn't you tell me before?"

Roger wasn't surprised she couldn't believe it. He found it difficult to believe himself. What were the chances, in all of this vast country, that he would have met the brother she sought? "Because I didn't know it was him. The man I met had a beard and mustache. And it never occurred to me your brother would be working as a ranch hand."

"A ranch hand?" The disbelief was evident in her eyes. "Where?"

"In Idaho. We met a few months ago. The son of the mayor of Gibeon got married and there was rather a large celebration in town. My gift to the bride and groom was a painting of the Tetons. Brian—your brother Grayson—learned I was the artist and introduced himself. Since coming to America and especially into this park, I've spoken with many aspiring artists, so that wasn't unusual. Your brother and I didn't talk at length, but he did show me a sketch he had with him. I daresay, it was of you."

If it was possible for her to look even more surprised, she did so now. "A sketch of me?"

"Yes, and now I understand why I had that familiar feeling when I first saw you. It was a good likeness. Not entirely you but close." He gave his head a slow shake. "I should have remembered that when I drew his likeness for you."

Tears swam before her hazel eyes. "It's a miracle," she said, almost too softly for him to hear.

Amanda reached for Victoria's hand. "It is, indeed, a miracle. Think of it, Roger. Miss Castleton would never have learned her brother's location if not for your chance meeting with him at a wedding in Gibeon and then the two of you meeting here in Yellowstone. God most surely directed her steps to you in answer to her prayers."

Chapter Eleven

E arly on Monday morning, the private coach carrying Victoria, Amanda, Isaiah, and Roger departed the Yellowstone Lake Hotel. The journey would take them first to Gardiner where they would bid farewell to the Coltranes, then head west and south into Idaho to a ranch called Eden's Gate. And after that to another ranch where her brother worked. In less than a week, she would see Grayson again. Was it truly possible? Had she actually found him? Only a few days ago she'd despaired of ever seeing him again. She'd thought she would be on her way back to Boston, alone, facing a life without any family. And now, because of the kindness and generosity of the man seated across from her, she would soon be reunited with the brother she so dearly loved.

Amanda Coltrane, Victoria learned, was not one to sit in silence for long. As the coach carried them north toward the junction near the Grand Canyon of the Yellowstone, she regaled Victoria with stories, beginning with the day her husband rescued her from a rushing river in the park. It amazed Victoria that a refined, well-spoken sister of a British lord had married a Yellowstone game scout. Even more amazing, Amanda now rode with Isaiah in the park, tracking poachers. What made her love that adventurous life? Not just adventurous. Dangerous! And it was ever so evident that Amanda *did* love it.

For herself, Victoria preferred structure. She liked to plan out her days, her weeks, her years. She was happiest with ordinary days, one day the same as the one before. It had been difficult enough, traveling across the country from Massachusetts to Montana. She couldn't imagine herself in Amanda's place, not even should she fall in love.

That thought drew her eyes toward Roger. He didn't appear to be listening to Amanda's chatter any longer. His gaze was fastened out the window of the coach at the passing countryside. Perhaps he wished he could stop the coach and sketch or paint something he saw through that window.

Amazement swept over her a second time as she thought about how Roger had changed his plans in order to help her. He had packed up all his art supplies, his completed paintings, everything he'd brought with him into Yellowstone, in order to escort her to Idaho. No one had asked him to do it. Certainly no one had compelled him. He had volunteered out of the goodness of his heart, and she would be forever grateful.

In some ways, he reminded her of Grayson. The creative side of their natures, the way they viewed the world around them, those were much the same. And yet they were quite different in other ways. Roger had a generous spirit, Grayson a selfish one. She'd spoiled her younger brother, and perhaps spoiling him was what made him thoughtless of others. Thoughtless of his own sister. So thoughtless he hadn't written to her in almost a year.

Emotions thickened her throat, and she lowered her gaze to her hands, now clasped tightly in her lap.

———

ROGER SAT BACK against the leather seat of the coach, watching the wilderness pass by. A pang of regret settled in his chest. He'd planned for a longer stay in the park. Weeks longer. More time to paint. More time to capture the ethereal beauty of Yellowstone. But God, it seemed, had dictated otherwise. And so here he was, just two weeks after his arrival, heading out of the park again.

And yet what other choice had he?

His gaze shifted to Victoria. Her eyes were downcast, and there was a sadness in her countenance that hadn't been there a short while before. He wondered what caused the change in her. It couldn't be Amanda's stories. No matter how dire the circumstances related in her tales, his young friend always managed to bring laughter to the mix. Perhaps Victoria was understandably worried about seeing her brother again after such a long time.

The coach slowed, letting them know they were nearing a change station. After they rolled to a stop,

Roger got out and helped the ladies down from the coach. Then he took a walk away from the road, stretching his legs and back in preparation for the next stage of their journey.

The scent of pine needles and damp earth mingled with the sulfuric tang from a distant hot spring. Through a stand of lodgepole pines, he saw the Yellowstone River and a small herd of bison grazing in clusters near its banks. He stopped to study them. The massive animals moved slowly as they nibbled, unperturbed and unthreatened, on grasses growing there. Meanwhile, a trumpeter swan glided on the river's surface, white wings catching the light of late morning.

Isaiah stepped to his side. After a short silence, he said, "'The heavens declare the glory of God; and the firmament sheweth his handywork.'"

Roger couldn't argue with the Scripture his friend quoted. The proof of it was right before their eyes.

"God sees your kindness to others, Roger."

He looked at Isaiah.

"Even I can see that leaving the park this early was a sacrifice. You planned a much longer stay."

Roger commented with a shrug.

"Perhaps it's more than mere kindness that takes you back to Idaho." A smile tugged at the corners of Isaiah's mouth.

Moments he'd spent in Victoria Castleton's company flashed in his mind. Her expressive eyes. Her tentative smile across a dinner table. The way she moved as she walked along the lakeshore. Her delight over one of his paintings. The sadness he'd seen on her countenance in the coach a short while before.

Isaiah gave Roger a pat on the back before walking away.

He turned his eyes toward the grazing bison once again. Great beasts that could move with surprising speed and agility, as he'd seen for himself the previous summer. He'd hoped to complete several paintings with the American buffalo as the focal point. Susannah Kennedy had inquired about just such a painting on Saturday, but alas, he had none to sell. However, she'd purchased four other paintings from him, two from the Grand Canyon of the Yellowstone and two from the lake. That was something, he supposed. And it wasn't as if he couldn't visit the park another time. He'd made the decision not to return to England. There would be other opportunities, surely. Perhaps even this fall.

But for now, there was Victoria. He didn't want to abandon her.

"Perhaps it's more than mere kindness . . ."

Isaiah was right about that. There were other reasons besides mere kindness, and it was pointless to deny it. He was attracted to Victoria. Far more than he wanted to be. Because there was no future in it. Roger had dreams for the future, and they didn't include settling in one place. Not yet. Maybe not ever.

He turned to walk back to the coach.

Victoria was sorry to say goodbye to Amanda and Isaiah in Gardiner the next evening. She suspected the coach would feel much too silent without the vivacious Mrs. Coltrane's company and more of her joyful stories. Not that she hadn't enjoyed her times with Roger, just the two of them, over the past couple of weeks. She had. But would that still be true as they traveled on together?

They departed Gardiner on Wednesday morning before the sun was fully up.

"We should be able to make it to the ranch before nightfall tomorrow," Roger told her. "Assuming nothing goes awry on the road."

Victoria's breath caught in her chest as she remembered the horrid sound and the rough jerk and sway of the stagecoach the day the wheel had broken. It was a wonder the coach hadn't ended up on its side. Or worse.

"These shall be rather long days," Roger continued, "but we'll be glad we pushed hard when we are able to spend the night in comfort again."

Still feeling a little breathless, she asked, "And when shall we go to see my brother?"

"I believe the Hasting Ranch is an hour or two south of Eden's Gate by wagon."

Her pulse quickened at that news. If all went well, she might see Grayson as early as Friday. It was almost too wonderful to believe. "Mr. Bernhardt, I am forever in your debt."

"Not at all. Not at all."

"No. Truly, sir. I am overwhelmed by your many kindnesses."

Something flickered across his face. An emotion she couldn't quite discern. And it made her heart beat even faster than the steady gallop of horses' hooves.

Chapter Twelve

L ate on the following day, as the coach bounced along the rough road, Roger recognized an oddly-twisted tree that grew beside an outcropping of rocks. It was so unique in appearance that, earlier in the summer, he'd spent a full morning sketching it from several different angles.

"We're nearly there," he said to Victoria.

"Truly?" Exhaustion written on her face, she grasped the edge of the open window on her right and leaned toward it to look out.

"We're on Overstreet land even now." He pointed through the opposite window. "Look. You can see some of the cattle."

She did as he suggested, sliding across the seat for a better view. "There are so many."

"And that's only a small part of the herd."

Victoria met his gaze. "I know nothing about ranch-ing. I've always lived in the city." A frown creased her brow. "I can't imagine Grayson working on a ranch. I could understand his desire to paint in Yellowstone. At least a little. He's always been passionate about art. But this—" She motioned with her hand. "I don't understand this. Why didn't he go back to Boston? Why did he come to Idaho instead of returning home?"

"I cannot say for certain, of course, but perhaps he fell in love with this part of the country the way I have. I'm sure there are many who knew me in England who don't understand my decision to remain."

"It isn't the same thing. You have no family to go back to. Grayson could have returned to his home where his sister waited for him."

"Then perhaps it was because of that young woman in his drawings. You said yourself you could see his affection for her in his work. Perhaps she is the reason he came to Idaho."

Her frown deepened. "That could be true, I suppose."

"Amanda stayed for love."

"For love," she whispered.

Her words seemed to twist in his chest, and after several heartbeats, he looked away, afraid that if he continued to stare into her eyes, he might do or say something he would regret.

Twenty minutes later, the coach rolled into the barnyard at Eden's Gate. As the rocking came to an end, Roger opened the door on his left and stepped to the ground. Then he helped Victoria do the same. As they faced the main house, he caught the surprise written in her eyes. Obviously she hadn't expected anything as grand as the L-shaped, three-story ranch house, its exterior covered in fieldstone of gray, white, and gold.

He looked toward the driver. "Donny, I'll see Miss Castleton inside, then be out to collect our belongings." With his hand beneath her elbow, he escorted Victoria toward the house.

The front door opened before they reached the porch and William stepped into view. He wore an equally surprised expression. "Roger?"

"Yes, it is I. And I daresay many weeks earlier than I told you."

"You're right about that. I didn't expect to see you until the end of September."

Roger glanced at Victoria. "This is Miss Castleton. I trust a room can be made available for her."

"Of course. Come in. I'll call for Mrs. Adler." He cocked an eyebrow in question an instant before disappearing into the house.

"Do not worry," Roger said softly. "You will be made very welcome for as long as you choose to stay." As the words left his mouth, he realized he hoped she would stay a good long while. Something else he might come to regret.

Inside the house, they were met by the housekeeper. Mrs. Adler wore her usual stern expression, but Roger was no longer put off by it. The woman's heart was as big as the Eden's Gate range. She loved fiercely and well, as he'd learned over the last fourteen months.

"Mr. Bernhardt, you were not expected." She clucked her tongue.

"I know, Mrs. Adler. I do apologize most strenuously. But I had good reasons for returning when I did." With a nod in Victoria's direction, he introduced her to the housekeeper.

"My dear Miss Castleton, you must be exhausted." Mrs. Adler motioned Victoria forward. "You come with me. We'll give you an opportunity to get washed and settled. Dinner will be on the table in another hour, but if you'd rather, I will bring a tray to your room."

"That's very kind, but a tray isn't necessary. I will come down for dinner. I don't want to put anyone out."

Mrs. Adler clucked her tongue a second time—the meaning unbeknownst to Roger—as she led Victoria away.

He gave his head a slight shake before turning toward the front door.

"What's going on?" William asked as he followed him outside. "Who is that woman?"

"It's a long story."

"I'll make the time to hear it."

"Let me tell you while I get my belongings unloaded. Also, can you put up the coachman for the night? Mr. Reardon has served me well, both going to Yellowstone and now on our early return."

"Of course there's room for him. He can stay in the guest cottage. It's empty."

"Thank you, William. Your hospitality is greatly appreciated."

VICTORIA REGRETTED REJECTING the offer of a dinner tray in her room. She longed to simply fall onto the bed and not move again until morning. Especially since the accommodations on this ranch exceeded anything she'd imagined. The room she'd been given was twice the size as the one she'd stayed in at the Yellowstone Lake Hotel, and the bed was wonderfully comfortable. So much so that it took great effort to rise from it to make herself presentable.

The travel dust brushed from her gown as much as possible, her face washed, and her hair tidied, she descended the stairs as a clock somewhere in the house chimed the hour. As if summoned by the sound, Roger appeared at the bottom of the staircase and offered his hand to take her the rest of the way. Delicious aromas wafted to her as they approached the dining room, making her realize her hunger.

Large windows looked out toward the Tetons, their granite heights lit by the evening sun. They made her feel small and insignificant by comparison. In her memory, she heard her mother's voice as she read aloud from her Bible: *"I will lift up mine eyes unto the hills, from whence cometh my help. My help cometh from the LORD, which made heaven and earth."*

Her mother's faith had been strong, despite the hardships she'd experienced—the loss of Victoria's father, then the loss of wealth and security during her second marriage. Despite it all, Claudette Castleton Townsend had trusted God to the very end of her life. She had believed He cared for her every thought and every breath. She'd believed the Lord cherished and loved her, and nothing had shaken that belief. Not ever.

Victoria wished she had the same kind of faith. She believed in God. She believed Jesus was the Christ, the Son of the Living God. But she wasn't sure God Almighty cared about every tiny detail. Didn't He help those who helped themselves? Which meant she needed to take control of her own life to make sure it didn't fall to pieces. That's what she'd been trying to do for more than a decade. Keep her world and her brother's world from falling to pieces. Trying and failing.

"Miss Castleton?"

She snapped back to the present and discovered Roger holding out a chair at the table, waiting expectantly. Feeling a flush of embarrassment rising in her cheeks, she settled onto it. Thankfully that was the moment their host entered the room. The men exchanged a few words as they took their own seats. Moments after that, Mrs. Adler came through a swinging door with a platter of roast beef. More serving bowls soon followed. Potatoes and gravy. Vegetables and breads.

When the housekeeper left for the final time, William said a blessing over the food, then lifted the nearest bowl and held it toward Victoria. "So, Miss Castleton. I understand you came west looking for your brother, and Roger here thinks he may be working for Major Hasting."

"That's his belief." She accepted the serving bowl, filled with peas and onions. "And my hope."

"I'll send one of the boys down to the Hasting

Ranch first thing in the morning to find out if your brother is there. If he is, we'll tell him you're at Eden's Gate. If he isn't there, we'll try to learn where he was headed after he left."

"That's good of you, Mr. Overstreet. Thank you."

"It does sound like God had a hand in putting you and Roger together," William continued as he slid several slices of roast beef onto his plate.

Her stomach tumbled at his choice of words. God may have arranged her meeting with Roger, but she would hardly say they'd been "put together." And yet . . . oddly enough, she had begun to think of him as being with her. Ridiculous, she was sure. He had done her a kindness. A great kindness. Several great kind-nesses. But there was surely no more to it than that. Nothing he had said or done made her think he had any interest in her other than as a gentleman helping a lady in distress.

Could she be wrong about that?

Chapter Thirteen

J uly heat beat down upon the ranch house and barnyard at midday. Victoria found shelter from the sun in the shade of the front porch, but anxiety made her too restless to sit for long. Instead she paced, her heart leaping at any sound that might possibly mean the approach of her brother. At the same time, she tried to prepare herself for more disappointment. Just because Grayson had been employed at that other ranch two or three months ago didn't mean he was still there.

But no. He had to be there. Surely the good Lord wouldn't have brought her to Eden's Gate in such an unexpected way only to take her brother away beforehand. Would He?

Please, Father. Please. Let Grayson be at that ranch. Let me see him. Perhaps make him come home with me. Please.

The sound of hoofbeats penetrated her thoughts. She moved to the porch railing, her hands gripping the wood as she waited.

Please, God. Please.

A cowboy on horseback rode into view. Disappointment sluiced through her. But then came a buggy. She moved toward the steps for a better view. Who was in the buggy? She had to see. Was it Grayson?

First she saw a young woman seated next to the driver, her hair covered with a straw hat. And then she saw the man holding the reins. Her breath caught. It was Grayson, and yet it hardly looked like him. He appeared older, his shoulders broader. His face and forearms had been darkened by the sun, and he'd grown a mustache and beard, just as Roger had said.

She hurried down the porch steps, emotion thickening her throat, and waited for her brother to get down from the buggy. After he did so, he rounded the back of the vehicle and tenderly helped the woman to the ground. A woman who was large with child. The woman from her brother's drawings. It was unmistakably her. And they were unmistakably in love.

Grayson turned in Victoria's direction. When their gazes met, he acknowledged her with a nod. Then he put an arm around the back of the woman at his side, and they walked toward Victoria. Questions flooded her mind. *How did you get here? Why didn't you come home to Boston? Why didn't you write to me?*

Her brother stopped a few feet away. "Hello, Vicky."

Tears welled in her eyes. "Grayson," she whispered. Saying his name seemed to break the invisible chains that had held her. She ran forward and threw her arms around him. "Oh, Grayson. You're all right. You're well."

He hugged her back. His mouth near her ear, he said, "I'm all right. I'm well."

"You didn't write." She drew her head back. "Why didn't you write?"

He cocked a brow. "You didn't answer the letters I sent to you. I thought you didn't want to hear from me. So I stopped writing."

Unexpected anger sparked as she took a couple of steps back from him. "I would have written if I'd known where you were. Your last letter said you were leaving Yellowstone soon and you didn't know where you were going from there."

"But I wrote after that. Twice." His voice rose slightly, matching Victoria's. "I told you where I was. But you never wrote again."

The woman at his side slipped a hand into the crook of his arm, perhaps a silent reminder of her presence.

Grayson drew a breath, his irritation instantly gone. "I'm sorry. I didn't know you never got those letters."

Victoria's questioning gaze went to the other woman. She looked to be about nineteen or twenty years old. She was pretty, in a rather simple way. Her face was round. Freckles dotted her nose and cheeks, and her blue eyes were lit with interest.

"Honey," Grayson said, "this is my sister, Victoria Castleton. Vicky, this is my wife, Kit Townsend."

Her brother had married without her knowing it. Without her being able to witness it. And they were expecting a baby. From the look of it, in a matter of weeks.

He won't be coming home with me. He's made a new life for himself.

The thought made her want to cry. Not tears of joy at seeing her brother again but tears of sorrow, of loneliness. She pictured her small, quiet home in Boston, the silence echoing around her because Grayson hadn't returned.

Her brother's gaze shifted to a spot over her right shoulder. Even before she turned to look, she knew Roger must have come out of the house. His arrival at her side came just in time to help her regain her composure.

He extended a hand to her brother. "Good to see you again, Mr. Townsend." They shook hands. "Do you go by Brian or Grayson?"

"Everyone calls me Brian these days." He looked at Victoria. "Think you can remember that?"

Strange, how the request felt like rejection. "I think I can, given a little time to get used to it."

"Thanks."

Tears threatened again.

"Why don't we all go inside." Roger cupped her elbow with a hand. "I daresay you two have a great deal to talk about."

Once again he'd saved her from giving in to her emotions. Bless him for that.

ONCE IN THE PARLOR, Brian introduced his wife to Roger. Then everyone took seats, Brian and Kit together on the sofa, Roger and Victoria in separate chairs. Mrs. Adler appeared out of the dining room with a tray holding glasses of lemonade.

"Thank you, Mrs. Adler." Roger stood, took the tray from her, and set it on the low table nearby.

"Is there anything else I can get for you, Mr. Bernhardt?"

"I don't believe so."

The housekeeper glanced at the couple on the sofa. "Will your guests be staying for lunch?"

He hadn't realized the time. "Jolly good idea, Mrs. Adler. We don't want them leaving with empty stomachs, not when it takes so long for them to get home again."

"We wouldn't want to put you out," Brian said.

Mrs. Adler made a sound in her throat that Roger interpreted to mean she was too prepared to be put out by anything asked of her. He grinned as he turned toward their guests again. "Then it is settled. You will dine with us."

Roger was about to regain his seat when it occurred to him that Victoria might want some private time with her brother and his wife. He was not family. He was, at most, a temporary host.

He cleared his throat as he reached for one of the glasses of lemonade. "If you will excuse me, I have a few matters to see to before lunch is served." With a nod toward Victoria, he strode from the parlor and down the short hallway to William's office. Once inside, he closed the door.

He had nothing else to do, of course. He'd awaited

the hoped-for arrival of Victoria's brother with almost as much anticipation as Victoria herself. It had pleased him to see the brother and sister embrace earlier, although he'd sensed tension between them too. He'd wanted to hear Brian's story, to learn what brought him to the Hasting Ranch from Yellowstone. Brian had obviously met the woman who was now his wife before he came to Idaho. How had they met? Where had they met? In Yellowstone or even before that? How long had they been married? So many questions. But just because he'd played a part in finding Brian Townsend did not give him the right to hear the answers. That was up to Victoria.

He went to the window of the office. Beyond the glass, tall trees stood like silent guards, no breeze stirring their leafy limbs. The heat of July and the lack of rain in recent weeks had changed the rolling landscape from the greens of spring to shades of gold and brown. He should paint this view in different seasons, he thought. His fingers itched to begin right now, but he had no supplies with him. If he left William's office, he would disturb whatever was happening in the parlor. He didn't want to do that. He didn't want anything to spoil this reunion for Victoria.

He hoped she knew that.

<hr>

Victoria listened as Grayson—no, Brian—shared the story of the past year. His time in Yellowstone. How he'd met Kit there, then how he'd followed her to Idaho where she was employed as a cook for Major Hasting. How they'd married in late fall and now awaited the birth of their baby around the first of September.

Brian lifted Kit's hand to his mouth and kissed the back of it. "We can't wait," he concluded.

It had occurred to Victoria, as Brian talked, that he had become a man before he left Boston, but she'd continued to think of him as a boy. Why hadn't she seen it? Look at him. A husband and soon to be a father. And the roles looked good on him. He was happy. Happy the way he'd been as a little boy before the harsh circumstances of life had encroached upon their family. Happier, even. Happier in a way she'd never experienced for herself.

The realization caused her chest to tighten.

"Now it's your turn, Vicky. Since you never got my letters, how on earth did you find me? In Idaho, of all places."

"God led me to you," she answered softly. "It is the only possible explanation."

Brian gave her a querying look.

She drew a breath and began to tell him her own story.

Chapter Fourteen

O n Sunday morning, Roger rode in the surrey beside William on their way to church. Behind them on the back seat were Mrs. Adler and Victoria. He wished he could have swapped places with the house-keeper. Victoria had been quiet and withdrawn since Friday's meeting with her brother and his wife. She'd appeared happy during lunch with Brian and Kit. But after the couple left, low spirits had seemed to wash over her and had stubbornly remained.

They'd covered about half the distance into Gibeon when William said, "I believe it's time I host another barbecue and barn dance at Eden's Gate. What say you to that?"

Roger answered, "That's a jolly good idea. How soon?"

"I can announce it at church today. We could do Saturday after next. That should be plenty of time for folks to plan to attend and for the news to spread." William glanced over his shoulder at the two women.

"You haven't said, Miss Castleton, but I assume you plan to remain on Eden's Gate until after the birth of your niece or nephew."

"I . . . I hadn't really thought about it. That is a long time for me to remain your guest. Five weeks at least my brother said."

"Not too long. Not at all. I rattle around in that big house alone most of the time. I appreciate the company."

Was that truly how William felt? If so, he could remedy it easily enough. A successful rancher in these parts—especially a young, good-looking one—could have his pick of single females. Last summer, Roger had wondered if William and Amanda might fall in love, but their relationship had never gone beyond friendship. Perhaps, if Victoria Castleton stayed at the ranch long enough, a romance might blossom between her and William.

That thought left an unpleasant taste in his mouth, and he knew why. Although he had no intention of acting upon his own attraction, he hated the idea of Victoria belonging to any other man. Not as long as he was still around. Wretchedly selfish of him, but it was the truth.

"Hey, Jake!" William called out, intruding on Roger's musings.

The ranch foreman trotted his horse closer to the surrey.

"Once we're in town, you and the boys help me spread the word. We're going to host another barbecue and dance at the ranch. Saturday after next."

"That'll please folks," Jake Foster said with a grin. "We'll be right glad to pass on the news. Especially since this time it didn't take catching rustlers to bring us all together."

"Rustlers?" Victoria inquired softly.

Mrs. Adler answered, telling what had transpired the previous summer with cattle thieves hitting the ranches up and down the range. "Once those vile men were tracked down, in no small part due to the help of Isaiah Coltrane, Mr. William hosted a barbecue and barn dance to celebrate the end of the trouble. And thank the good Lord, there's been no such trouble this year."

William chuckled. "Amen to that, Mrs. Adler. Amen to that."

The surrey crested a rise, and the white clapboard church on the eastern edge of Gibeon came into view. The church looked like other churches Roger had seen on his visits to Washington, western Idaho, and Montana over the past year and a half. For that matter, the town of Gibeon looked quite like other small towns he'd stayed in or passed through. Main streets bordered by restaurants and sheriff's offices, newspapers and general stores, hotels and boarding houses, saloons and liveries. The people in these American towns in the West were independent and strong-minded. They had stories to tell from their pasts and dreams for their futures to fight for. Many of them—perhaps most—had a faith in God that never seemed to waver. Good people in a good land. He liked them, these Americans. Liked them a lot. Enough to want to become one of them.

The surrey was brought to a halt in a shaded area

beneath some tall trees. While William tied the horse to a hitching post, Roger helped the ladies to the ground.

"Come with me, Miss Castleton," Mrs. Adler said in that no-nonsense manner of hers. "I'll introduce you to the good reverend."

He felt a stab in his gut. Truman Blankenship, the pastor of Gibeon Chapel, was another bachelor in the valley who might take an interest in Victoria. He was both wise and kind. A good man, deserving of a good woman. How could he not be interested in her?

Roger and William fell into step behind the two women, close enough to hear Mrs. Adler say, "We are so blessed that Reverend Blankenship came to live in Gibeon. A circuit preacher tended to this flock before that, but that meant services were sporadic. Now we pray the reverend will take himself a wife and raise a family here."

Roger's jaw clenched.

"So that's the way of it," William said in a low voice.

"Way of what?"

His friend answered with a bark of laughter that drew gazes from several quarters.

A wave of shock passed through Roger as he realized another truth. He wasn't simply selfish. He was jealous. But that was preposterous. He had no interest in romance—with Victoria or any other woman. Marriage had been his father's goal for him, along with the running of the drapery business in London. With the business sold, there was no need for him to settle in one place. He had the funds to continue his untethered way of life for years to come, as long as he wasn't reckless.

He could see more of this great land. He'd already decided this would be his last winter in Idaho. In the spring, he would make his way toward the Pacific Ocean. He would stop and paint any time he saw something that appealed to him, and he would move on when the spirit moved him.

That was the life he wanted. That was the life he would have. And no woman would change his mind about it. Not even one as fetching as Victoria Castleton.

***

"So NICE TO MEET YOU, Reverend Blankenship." Victoria shook the pastor's hand and turned to enter the church through the front double doors when she saw her brother ride up to the churchyard. She excused herself and stepped away from the others, waiting for Grayson to join her. She drew in a breath, mentally correcting herself. Brian. She must remember to call him Brian.

As he approached, she noticed again the breadth of his shoulders, the confident way he carried himself, the easy smile that curved his mouth. He'd made a new life in this rugged country full of wide open spaces, while her life in Boston had remained the same. The way she liked it. Full of routine and familiarity.

Routine and familiarity *was* the way she liked it. Wasn't it?

Brian stopped before her and gave her cheek a quick peck.

"I wasn't sure I would see you today," she said.

"It's a long way to Gibeon from the Hasting Ranch.

Too far really. Almost three hours by wagon. That's why Kit isn't with me. She's done in from the trip up and back to see you at Eden's Gate. The major holds his own little service on Sundays for those who want to take part."

"Do you like working for him?"

"I do." He offered his arm. "He's a good man. Bit rough around the edges but fair. I like the men I work with too. I didn't know how well I'd fit in when I followed Kit to Idaho. But I fit. I like the work, the way of life. Never dreamed that would be true, but it's right for me."

Victoria felt a twinge of envy. Her brother had come to Idaho because he fell in love, and he'd made a new life for himself, a life that suited him. Not everyone was so lucky.

"Have you decided how long you intend to stay?" he asked as they moved toward the church entrance.

"Mr. Overstreet invited me to remain his guest until after your child is born."

His grin broadened. "That's good to hear. You'll do it, won't you? You'll stay."

"I . . . I haven't decided."

"You need to stay, sis. I want you here. I'll need you with me when the baby comes."

Although she didn't admit it to him, those words were enough to make up her mind. She would remain in Idaho until the end of summer.

Chapter Fifteen

As the buggy crested a rise in the land three days later, Victoria got her first good view of the Hasting Ranch.

The two-story house was built of logs and was, at most, a third the size of the house on Eden's Gate. There was a barn and a bunkhouse but no other outbuildings. Everything about the place looked rougher and lesser than the ranch belonging to William Overstreet. It shouldn't surprise her but it did. For some reason, she'd expected all ranches to be the same in the area. Not that she had any real knowledge of ranching, here in Idaho or elsewhere.

She glanced at Roger. "Thank you again for doing this." It seemed she was constantly thanking this man. He had done so much for her in the last month. Words of thanks felt like too little, but they were all she had to offer.

"I was glad to do it. I haven't passed down this way for more than a year."

"You don't know the major well?"

"No." He shook his head, his gaze remaining on the road ahead. "I met him at the barn dance last September, and we talked some. That's the only time we've met."

"Is there a Mrs. Hasting?"

"I heard she died about ten years ago. He's got a daughter in Texas. She lives there with her husband and four children. But the major told me he means to be buried on his ranch. I guess he doesn't mind having no family nearby."

"But you don't know him well," she commented.

Roger's eyebrows arched, then he laughed. "Touché."

"I'm sorry." She looked away, embarrassed that she'd spoken to him thus. "That was rude of me."

"Not rude at all, Miss Castleton, for it is true. I am a keen observer and a good listener. Or so I have been told."

"And you remember. You remembered my brother."

"Eventually." Roger drove the buggy into the barnyard of the Hasting Ranch and pulled the horse to a stop, ending their conversation.

Brian and Kit must have been waiting for them. Before Roger could step to the ground, Victoria's brother and his wife were already walking toward the buggy.

"We're glad you could come." Brian offered a hand to help Victoria down. "Come on inside. Kit's got something cool for you to drink after that long drive."

The barnyard was quiet. A couple of horses stood

in a nearby corral, their heads hanging low, their tails swishing slowly. A hound slept in the shade beneath the front porch, apparently undisturbed by their arrival.

Kit moved awkwardly to Victoria's free side, one hand resting on the swell of her belly. Together they walked toward the house. "The major said he would join us for lunch. He's out on the range this morning but should return soon. While we wait for him, I'll show you around."

Victoria cast a glance in her brother's direction as her sister-in-law drew her into the house. A rich aroma tickled her nose, the scent of onions and beef. They passed through a parlor crowded with chairs and a settee. The dining area beyond the front parlor had a large table with benches on the long sides and straight-backed chairs on either end. The table was already set for five people. The kitchen was large, although not as large as the one at Eden's Gate, and the delicious aroma was much stronger here, a large pot on the stovetop holding whatever would be served for lunch.

Kit opened a door off the kitchen. "And this is our little place."

Looking in, Victoria saw a small sitting room and, beyond it, an open door revealed a bedroom.

"Come and see the cradle Brian made for the baby."

"He built a cradle?"

Kit nodded.

Victoria didn't remember her brother building anything. He'd never exhibited an interest in doing things with his hands other than with a pencil or paintbrush. When had he learned to make furniture, even something as small as a cradle?

Kit led the way into the bedroom. Leaning over, she lovingly stroked the wooden railing of the cradle, setting it to rocking. "Isn't it beautiful?"

"Yes," Victoria whispered in response. Love had crafted the cradle, far more than knowledge or ability or talent. Brian had made this bed for his child and wife out of love, and it would have been beautiful even if it had been full of flaws and mistakes. Which it wasn't.

Kit straightened. "I'm so glad you're here. Brian's missed you something awful, and it near broke his heart when he thought you didn't want to hear from him anymore." She held out a hand. "I always wanted a sister, Victoria. I hope you'll be mine."

A lump tightened her throat and tears welled in her eyes. "I … I will be so gladly," she managed to answer, surprised by her own emotional response.

As soon as they were out of the small apartment, Kit looped her arm with Victoria's so that they walked the remaining way to the parlor side-by-side. The gesture felt both strange and comforting.

When the Castleton fortune had been lost, when the Townsend family had been forced from the Boston mansion, Victoria had found herself without friends as well. The girls she'd known her entire life had disappeared as quickly as the security that once enveloped her. But now there was a young woman who wanted to not only be her friend but her sister as well.

Strange and comforting.

As Victoria and Kit re-entered the parlor a short

while later, in time to see the front door open and the man Victoria assumed was the major enter the house—a man in his sixties with a full beard and bushy eyebrows. The hair on his head, unruly from the hat he'd worn, was thick and as white as snow.

"Looks like I didn't miss lunch," he said. Then he lifted his chin and sniffed the air. "Smells good, whatever it is. I say, let's eat."

As Kit set bowls filled with a thick stew before each person at the table, steam curling upward, Roger's mouth watered, his hunger sharpened by the tantalizing aroma of beef and caramelized onions. He'd been hungry before. Now he felt ravenous.

"Let's bless the food so we can dig in," the major said from the chair at the head of the table. Wasting no time, he bowed his head and repeated a quick grace.

After the amen, Roger opened his eyes, his gaze on the large bowl before him. Swimming in the base were chunks of potatoes, carrots, and celery. Unless his nose deceived him, Kit had added herbs to the mixture—thyme, perhaps, and bay leaves. The scent reminded him of evenings spent around his mother's table back in London when he was a lad. Odd, he hadn't thought of that in years.

Kit, seated beside Brian on the bench opposite Roger and Victoria, held a plate of sliced bread toward him. "It came out of the oven not long before you arrived."

Roger took a couple of slices and buttered them generously. When he looked up again, ready to make some comment, something told him that conversation over a meal wasn't expected at this particular table. Perhaps it wouldn't even be welcomed. And so, like the others, he focused his attention on the stew and began to eat.

As the silence lengthened, Roger thought of his father. Peter Bernhardt had preferred a quiet mealtime as well. He had come to the table to eat, not to converse with his wife and son. He had eaten, then excused himself and returned to his business. And there had always been more business to attend to. He remembered his mother, that look of loneliness that had crossed her face so often. Roger had felt the loneliness too. His father hadn't been unkind. Simply unaware. Distant. Preoccupied. He'd wanted to succeed, to build a business, to provide well for his family. But in his effort to provide, he'd had no time remaining to spend with that very same family. When Roger's mum passed away, it seemed to him that his father scarcely noticed her absence.

He swallowed his last bite of stew and set the spoon in the empty bowl, the clink of metal meeting earthenware seeming much too loud in the room. In response, the four others at the table looked in his direction.

"It was very good, Mrs. Townsend," Roger said. "Thank you."

The major wiped his mouth with a napkin. "It was delicious, indeed. As always. I've never had a better cook in my kitchen."

A blush rose in Kit's cheeks.

Brian Townsend was a fortunate man, Roger thought. He'd found a new way of life that suited him and gained a woman who loved him in the process.

He glanced toward Victoria. She wore a strange expression. A look of confusion, perhaps. And was it any wonder? In the many months she and her brother had been separated, Grayson had become Brian, a boy had become a man, a brother had become a husband and soon-to-be father, an artist had become a cowboy. Drastic changes.

Would Victoria be willing to make similar changes in her own life? As if hearing Roger's silent question, she turned her gaze in his direction, and he feared her answer would be no. But in that moment, he found himself wishing he could change her mind.

Chapter Sixteen

Victoria awakened early the following morning, her thoughts immediately churning even before her eyes opened to watch as dawn chased the shadows of night away.

Perhaps a little more than a month until her brother's baby was born. And then what? Would she remain until the christening? Longer? Not that long? She would return to Boston. But to what?

The major's ranch was two hours away by buggy. Too far for her to go down every day. Besides, her brother had work to do. So did Kit. So how often would she get to see them while she was in Idaho? The major had no spare room for her to stay in, and in truth, she wouldn't feel as welcome there as she did in the Overstreet home, even if she'd been asked. Still, she was remaining in Idaho to spend time with Brian and his little family, and yet she was too far away to do much of that.

What was she to do with her days when she wasn't

with them? Chuck Kincaid wouldn't want her in the kitchen—unlike Kit, Victoria wasn't a good cook—and Mrs. Adler had been quick to decline her offers to help elsewhere in the house. While she loved to read, she didn't want to do that for hours and hours every day. Roger's image came to mind, but she pushed it away. She couldn't impose herself on him any more than she already had. After all, she wasn't his responsibility, despite how safe he made her feel. Safe and valued.

Dear Roger . . .

Letting out a breath, she rolled onto her side. As she did so, she recalled the cradle Brian had made for his baby. That little bed would surely need linens and blankets, and the infant would need clothes. "I could knit a blanket. I could knit several." She sat up with a sudden burst of energy. "And I can sew clothes as well."

Smiling to herself, she rose and prepared for the day ahead, eager to find William so she could ask him about using a horse and buggy to go into town. Thankfully she didn't need someone to drive her there. Although she hadn't been able to keep a horse in recent years, her stepfather had taught her to drive a buggy when she was still a young girl. It wasn't something she'd forgotten how to do. And she knew the way into Gibeon. There was only one road, and it was without twists and turns or forks to confuse her.

Fortunately for Victoria, the Overstreet household rose early. She didn't have to wait long for William to appear in the dining room, followed soon after by Roger. As soon as all three were seated—plates of sausage and biscuits as well as a bowl of gravy before them—she looked toward her host. "Mr. Overstreet, I wondered if I might have use of a horse and buggy today. I would like to go into Gibeon."

"Of course. You may take them whenever you wish, Miss Castleton. There's usually one of the men available to help harness a horse for you."

"Thank you. That's good of you."

As he cut into a sausage patty with his fork, Roger asked, "What is it that takes you into town? If you don't mind sharing."

"I want to buy some yarn and knitting needles. Perhaps some fabric too. To make a few things for the baby."

"I'm sure Kit will be appreciative. She said she still needed many items before the birth." He gave his head a shake. "But you wouldn't have heard her. You and Brian were outside when she mentioned it. Seems she is excellent in the kitchen but not so much with needle and thread."

Pleasure welled in Victoria's heart. She'd liked the idea of knitting a blanket and a sweater for her niece or nephew, but knowing these things were needed made her plans all the sweeter.

"Would you mind if I accompanied you into town?" Roger asked. "I would like to place an order for some art supplies. I planned to do it in the next week or two, but I might as well do it today."

Her stomach fluttered in anticipation, and she realized she had hoped for that very request. She could have gone alone. She would have gone alone. But how much better to go with Roger.

Dear Roger . . .

The fluttering intensified. That was the second time in less than two hours that those words had played through her mind, and she realized in that moment how much meaning was wrapped up in them.

Dear Roger . . .

He'd become ever so much more to her than the kind man who had done her favor upon favor. She noticed his absence when he wasn't with her. She looked forward to the first sight of him at breakfast in the morning, and the last sight of him before she went up to her bedchamber in the evening. There was something about the blue of his eyes and the tousled look of his blond hair and the way one corner of his mouth curved upward, hinting at a smile even when it didn't fully become one.

"Miss Castleton?"

She blinked, brought out of her private thoughts. "I'm sorry. What did you say?"

"I asked if I might accompany you to town."

"Oh. Yes. Of course." She felt heat rising in her cheeks. "That is perfectly all right. I will . . . I will be happy to have your company."

FROM THE FIRST moment he'd seen it, Roger had loved the countryside that surrounded Eden's Gate, a land of sagebrush and pine trees that gently rolled like a calm sea until it swept up into the foothills at the base of the jagged mountains. So unlike the land of his birth. Both beautiful in their own unique ways.

Now, the green grasses of spring had turned golden as July prepared to change to August. It had been weeks since a storm had brought rain to the rangeland. Drought had become a word on the lips of more than one ranch hand, and Roger had noticed the worry creeping into William's eyes whenever he looked at the clear blue of the sky.

Roger thought of his friend's worries as the buggy carried him and Victoria toward Gibeon. The breeze created by the forward motion was warm upon his face, promising another hot and dry day.

Lord God, we could use some rain.

"You are deep in thought, Mr. Bernhardt."

He glanced at Victoria. "I was praying for rain."

One of her eyebrows arched.

"The creeks have started to run low."

Now she frowned. "I didn't know."

"I daresay it isn't serious yet. But without rain soon, it will become so. At least, that's what the men have told me."

"I fear I've been so wrapped up in my own concerns I haven't noticed the concerns of others." She turned her head to look at the passing landscape. "I must do better."

She spoke the last words softly, but he heard her all the same. Heard her and was prepared to tell her she judged herself too harshly. But Gibeon came into view just then, and her demeanor brightened.

He drove the horse directly to the mercantile. A

short while later, Victoria was considering the selection of yarns and fabrics offered, and Roger was giving a written list of art supplies to Harry Hathaway, the proprietor.

"I'll get these ordered straight away, Mr. Bernhardt. My supplier in Chicago should be able to get it all to me in about three weeks. Maybe a little less."

"Three weeks should be fine."

Harry held up an index finger. "Come to think of it. I've got a letter for you waiting with the rest of the Eden's Gate mail."

"News from Sebastian, I presume."

"No, sirree. Didn't come from England. It come from some place back east. I noticed. I'll get it for you, along with the rest of the ranch mail."

From someone in the east? He couldn't imagine who that would be.

While he waited for the proprietor to return from the room that served as the Gibeon post office, Roger turned his back to the counter and observed Victoria as she placed several skeins of cream-colored yarn in a basket. There was a tenderness in her expression that tugged at his chest. He suspected she imagined the infant who one day would be wrapped in the blanket she made with her purchase. She would love that child as she loved the child's father. But she would be so far away. Why did she feel the need to return to Boston? From what he understood, there was no other family there?

"Here you go, Mr. Bernhardt."

He faced the counter again.

Harry held out the letter. "See. I was right. Come from Rhode Island. It says so on the postmark."

Rhode Island? Susannah and Howard Kennedy were from Rhode Island. But there hadn't been time enough for them to return to their home in Providence and then write to him. Distracted, he mumbled his thanks, then walked out of the mercantile. Standing beside the buggy, he opened the envelope and pulled out the paper within. The letterhead—in bold, black letters—read, THE WHITAKER GALLERY.

His heart stuttered as he began to read:

Dear Mr. Bernhardt,

I am writing to you on behalf of Mr. and Mrs. Kennedy whom you met in Yellowstone National Park. Mr. and Mrs. Kennedy are patrons of the arts in Providence and have been faithful benefactors of The Whitaker Gallery for many, many years. It is the desire of Mrs. Kennedy that the gallery acquire five more of your paintings to be put on display. She has authorized me to purchase them, sight unseen, stating that she trusts you to already know her preferences. These paintings do not need to be from your time in Yellowstone alone. Anything that represents the West will satisfy her. Although she did mention a desire for one to be of a bison. The Whitaker Gallery will pay for the shipping as well.

Sincerely,
Algernon Whitaker

The words seemed to blur on the page, and Roger

blinked to clear his vision, not believing what he'd read so far. Five more paintings. Sight unseen. A gallery showing.

Where exactly was Providence, Rhode Island? He hadn't a clue, other than it was on the eastern side of this vast country. But his works were to be on display there. A showing in a gallery. Something he'd secretly desired for years but had never given voice to.

He thought of the day—had it been two weeks before?—when Mrs. Kennedy saw his paintings from the Grand Canyon of the Yellowstone. If the stagecoach hadn't arrived at just the right time. If the crate hadn't been dropped. If the paintings hadn't been exposed by the mishap. He hadn't known the Kennedys were patrons of the arts. Not even after they'd purchased several of his paintings.

Mrs. Kennedy wanted a painting of a bison. Somehow he would give her one. He'd made sketches of the great beasts. He would work from those. And if he wasn't satisfied with the results, he would have to return to the park. Perhaps he never should have left it.

He heard the small bell that announced the opening of the mercantile door and turned toward the sound. Victoria was there, her purchases filling the small basket on her arm. And he wondered if he could have allowed her to leave Yellowstone without him. Even for the sake of his art.

Chapter Seventeen

Victoria stood before the mirror in the bedroom, checking her appearance one final time. Excitement tumbled in her belly. It had been building inside of her for more than a week as everyone at the ranch—William, Roger, Mrs. Adler, the cook, all the cowboys, and Victoria herself—prepared for the barbecue and barn dance. Celebrations such as this hadn't been part of her own experience in Boston. If not for the disastrous loss of the family fortune, Victoria would have attended balls and soirees and other society outings for young ladies of her class. But those expectations had ended before she came of age, well before the deaths of her mother and stepfather.

Social class and money, or the lack thereof, didn't matter on this night and in this place. Everyone who lived within riding distance of Eden's Gate Ranch had been invited to the event—rich and poor, young and old —and from what she'd been told, there wouldn't be many who didn't come. Victoria couldn't wait to experience it for herself.

She went down the stairs and made her way to the kitchen. Mrs. Adler was lifting a large bowl of potato salad off the work table as Victoria entered the room.

"Let me help you with that," she said, hurrying forward.

"Thank you, dear. Folks are starting to arrive, and I haven't begun to get all the food onto the tables." The woman looked as harried as she sounded.

Victoria took the heavy bowl and moved toward the back door. "I'll be right back to help with the rest."

Outside, tables had been set up beneath the branches of tall trees. The air was filled with the scent of grilling meats. Unlit lanterns hung throughout the barnyard, waiting for dusk to blanket the earth. Guests had, indeed, begun to arrive, and they milled about, greeting one another and chatting in small groups.

"Miss Castleton." Roger's warm voice came from just behind her.

She started and turned.

"Let me have that." He took the bowl and set it on the nearest table. "You should be enjoying yourself."

"Mrs. Adler needs help."

He nodded. "All right. Help I can provide." He looked over his shoulder and motioned with one hand. Moments later, several Eden's Gate cowboys joined them.

If Mrs. Adler was surprised to see Victoria return with a group of men, she didn't show it. Instead, she barked directions to each one of them, and in no time at all, the prepared bowls and platters of food—coleslaw, pickled beets, cornbread, fried potatoes, baked beans, pies, cakes, and more—had been lifted off the work table and counter and carried outside.

"What else can I do?" Victoria asked as the last man disappeared through the back door.

"Not a thing." Mrs. Adler flicked her hand in a shooing motion. "You go on now and enjoy yourself. I plan to do the same."

She obliged without argument and arrived outside just as the buggy from the Hasting Ranch pulled into the barnyard. Smiling, she hurried to greet Brian and Kit. After helping his wife to the ground, Brian embraced Victoria, then stepped back to look at her while still holding her by the upper arms.

"Don't you look as pretty as a calf in clover," he said, his grin revealing dimples in his bearded cheeks.

Victoria laughed softly. A month ago, she would have thought the words ridiculous, especially coming from him. But not now. "I suppose, since you did say pretty, that I'll accept it as a compliment."

"I meant it as one."

Kit placed a hand on the small of her back and grimaced.

Brian's expression changed to a look of concern. "Let's find you a place to sit in comfort."

"I don't think there is any such place," she answered. "Not the comfortable part, at least. But I'll be glad to sit on something that isn't moving."

Victoria had little experience with women who were in the family way, but she thought Kit looked particularly miserable today. Her face was red and splotchy with beads of sweat forming along her hairline. If not for Brian's arm around her back, she might not have managed to get to a bench in the shade of the barn.

"May I get you something to drink?" Victoria asked once her sister-in-law was settled.

"Please. I am parched from the long ride."

She hurried to oblige, and after she returned with a glass of punch, she moved to stand beside her brother. "Maybe you shouldn't have come," she said softly.

"I thought the same." He gave his head a slight shake. "But Kit insisted she was not going to be the only one for miles around to miss the festivities. She promised me she felt fine when we left the ranch."

"I hate the thought of your long trip home in the dark."

"The moon'll be up and full by the time we leave, and the horse knows the way. We'll be fine."

Hoping he was right, Victoria went to sit beside Kit on the bench. After a short while, Brian was drawn away to stand with a group of other cowboys.

"I still can't get used to seeing him that way," she said, more to herself than to Kit.

"What way?"

"You know. Dressed like the other ranch hands in denims and boots. At ease with them. As if he's been riding horses and roping cattle since he was a boy."

"He didn't look like that when we first met."

Victoria glanced over at Kit.

Her sister-in-law smiled. "He was a dude if ever I saw one. Still wore a vest and a tie. That was not far from the Lake Hotel. He'd laid aside his suit coat because the day was warm, and the sleeves of his shirt were rolled up to his elbows. He sat on a boulder at the water's edge while he sketched a swan floating by him. He was the most handsome man I'd ever laid eyes on. I thought so then. I think so now."

Victoria agreed with Kit that her brother was a handsome man. But the most handsome? She looked for and found Roger among the people milling about the barnyard, and she knew she would never think any man more handsome than he.

CLOSE TO TWO hours after the first of the Eden's Gate guests arrived, Roger slipped away from the crowd to stand by himself, shoulder leaning against a gnarled tree trunk. He'd had his fill of both food and conversation, at least for a few moments.

Across the barnyard, Sheriff Frank Lewis was having an animated conversation with Reverend Truman Blankenship. The sheriff had a good twenty years on the pastor, but Truman could hold his own, no matter the topic of discussion.

Not far from those two men, William stood at a corral fence, facing the Tetons, the rocky peaks splashed with pinks and purples as the sun lowered in the western sky. Other men stood with him, and Roger suspected they were talking about the weather once again. About rain and the lack thereof.

A couple of the Eden's Gate cowboys began to light

the many lanterns that had been hung around the barn-yard, and the strumming of a banjo could be heard coming from inside the barn. If the musicians were getting ready, it wouldn't be long before the dancing began.

His thoughts went back in time to the previous September, to another barbecue and barn dance. He remembered sitting beside Amanda, watching as others whirled around the center of the barn in time to the music. He remembered saying that the Americans knew how to throw a good party. And he remembered dancing with her—but only because the man she truly wanted to dance with had a broken ankle.

Come to think of it, he'd danced with quite a few of the women present that night. Young and middle-aged. Single and married. Laughing and dour-faced. He'd enjoyed them all. But tonight? Tonight there was only one woman he cared to partner with, and his gaze sought her out now.

Victoria was once again seated on a bench beside her sister-in-law. In fact, Victoria had spent most of the last two hours with Kit, making sure the expectant woman had whatever she needed. He was glad the two of them got along well. However, he didn't want Victoria to stay there once the dancing started. Tonight was his opportunity to hold her in his arms. Something he'd wanted to do far longer than he cared to admit.

Time for Kit's husband to take over.

He found Brian seated with Major Hasting on the front porch of the house. The major puffed on a cigar, then sipped a beverage that definitely wasn't the punch being served by Mrs. Adler.

"Care to join us?" Brian asked as Roger stopped at the bottom of the steps.

"Thank you, but no. The dancing is about to begin, and I thought you might want to escort your wife into the barn so she can watch while listening to the music."

Perhaps Brian saw through to the real reason behind his suggestion. Roger didn't care. As long as Victoria didn't have an excuse to refuse him when he asked her to dance, that's what mattered.

"Good idea." Brian stood. "Major, if you'll excuse us."

"Of course. Of course. You young folks go have a good time."

People were now moving in the direction of the open barn doors, a lively tune inviting them inside. Roger and Brian cut through the crowd on their way to the bench where Victoria sat with Kit. Upon seeing the men's approach, Victoria smiled. Perhaps she'd been wishing for this moment. He hoped so.

He stopped before her. "Miss Castleton, I hoped you might join me for a dance." He held out a hand.

She glanced at the woman beside her.

"Don't worry, Vicky. I'll be with Kit." Brian took a seat on the opposite side of his wife.

Victoria placed her fingers in Roger's hand, color rising in her cheeks. With a gentle tug, he drew her to her feet, then moved her hand to the crook of his arm. "You're going to enjoy this."

Moments later, they paused in the barn doorway to

observe the festivities. The musicians—five men of various ages playing a fiddle, a banjo, a couple of guitars, and a harmonica—sat or stood on a raised platform at the far end of the building. Couples spun around the center of the barn in time to a lively polka, the women's skirts flying up to reveal white petticoats beneath. Around the circumference of the barn, people sat on chairs, barrels, and bales of straw.

Victoria looked at Roger, a worried expression in her eyes. "I'm afraid I've never danced like that."

"Not to worry. I learned that if you laugh and spin fast enough, no one cares if you know the steps or not."

Her look of concern didn't change.

He lowered his voice. "We'll wait for a slower number. A waltz, perhaps?"

She smiled in relief.

To be honest, he preferred to wait for a slow dance himself. For that meant holding Victoria closer.

Chapter Eighteen

Victoria and Roger had been inside the barn no more than a few minutes when the first lilting notes of "The Blue Danube" rose like a breath of wind. It wasn't the grand sweep of violins as she'd once heard in a Boston concert hall, but the fiddler played with a kind of aching devotion that made the old waltz shimmer all the same. The noise and laughter that had filled the barn hushed as the melody unfolded like a river at twilight—slow and elegant, with turns that stirred the heart before gently carrying it downstream.

Somehow, she found herself in Roger's arms as they began to turn across the floor in time to the one-two-three, one-two-three rhythm. There was nothing polished about the moment. The boards beneath her feet creaked, lantern light flickered across rough beams, and the scent of barbecued beef clung to the air. But still, the music wrapped around her like silk. She closed her eyes for a heartbeat and let herself believe she was dancing in Vienna. Or perhaps not

Vienna at all, but a place between worlds—where dreams floated like mist and every step was a promise waiting to be kept.

But Victoria was too practical to allow her thoughts to remain so far from reality. She had given up girlhood dreams long ago. Even "The Blue Danube" and being held in Roger's arms couldn't keep her there.

She opened her eyes, looking up into his handsome face. He watched her, his expression tender and caring, and she feared the emotions that shot through her in response. This man was unfettered. He no longer had a home. Not in England. Not in America. That didn't seem to bother him. Yes, he had talent, and yes, he'd sold some of his paintings. But being an artist didn't offer a life of security. And above all else, Victoria longed to feel secure. To know what tomorrow held in store for her. That mattered more to her than anything else.

The last strains of the song drifted through the air. The turning about the dance floor stopped. Couples applauded the musicians before drifting from the center of the barn.

"One more dance?" Roger asked softly.

She opened her mouth, not even sure what she was about to say, but before she could speak, her brother's voice intruded.

"Vicky, come quick. It's Kit. Something's wrong."

Victoria met Roger's gaze for a second before turning and hurrying after Brian. When she arrived at the bench where she'd left the couple not so very long before—at least she didn't think it had been long—she saw Kit, eyes closed, mouth set, perspiration dripping down the sides of her face.

"Kit?"

Her sister-in-law opened her eyes. "It hurts," she said through a clenched jaw. "Bad."

Victoria gave her head a shake. She wasn't sure why Brian had come for her. She couldn't do anything about—

Wait. Kit was in pain. Could it be . . . labor? But it was too soon for that.

She looked at Brian and saw Roger standing just beyond him. "Find Dr. Grant. Tell him it looks like the baby is coming. And get Mrs. Adler. We'll need her too."

Roger was gone in a moment.

"Brian, we must get her inside." She leaned close to Kit. "Can you walk?"

Kit nodded, her eyes closed again, a low groan escaping her lips. But when she tried to stand a few heartbeats later, she cried out and fell back onto the bench with a soft thud.

Brian didn't hesitate. He slid an arm beneath Kit's knees and placed his other arm behind her back. "Grab my neck, honey. You hear me? Grab my neck. There we go."

"Follow me." Victoria spun away from the bench and headed toward the front porch.

Few of the Overstreet guests remained outdoors, and those who did seemed unaware that anything was wrong as Victoria and Brian, with Kit in his arms, hurried across the barnyard. The same was not true for the major. He stood as they approached and—seeming to understand the situation at once—moved to open the front door.

"Thank you, sir," Victoria said as they swept past him.

"Where should I take her?" Brian asked.

At that moment, Mrs. Adler—followed by Roger—rushed into the parlor. "Up the stairs. The room to the left." She pointed before looking over her shoulder. "Mr. Bernhardt, have Mr. Kincaid put on water to boil. Then see what's keeping Dr. Grant."

Victoria led the way up the stairs, and once in the bedroom, she pulled back the bed coverings so Brian could lay his wife on the mattress. Soon after, the doctor entered the room, black bag in hand.

"I hear tell that a baby may be on its way," he said. His demeanor calmed Victoria.

But Kit shook her head. "It's too soon. I've got three weeks to go yet."

"Well, we'll see about that. Babies don't always arrive by our time schedules." The doctor looked at Brian, who stood anxiously off to one side. "Mr. Townsend, I think it might be best if you waited downstairs. Nervous husbands aren't much good at times like these."

"But—"

Kit groaned.

"Go on now." Dr. Grant set his bag on a nearby ladder-back chair, his gaze focused on his patient.

Victoria took her brother by the arm and urged him gently toward the door. "It's all right, Grayson." She hesitated but didn't bother to correct herself. It didn't seem important, given the situation. Giving him a tiny push, she added, "I'll come for you if you're needed. I promise."

Part of her wished she could go with him. She couldn't imagine she would be of much use to the doctor. But since he hadn't ordered her away, she would stay. At the very least, she could pray for it all to go well and be a support for Kit.

THE CLOCK on the parlor mantel kept time with a maddening steadiness, each tick counting the seconds that stretched out like taut wire.

Roger sat stiffly on the edge of the parlor settee, the toe of his boot tapping a faint, erratic rhythm against the hardwood floor. The sound of fiddle music floated in through the open windows—cheerful, unknowing strains from the barn where lanterns glowed and laughter still rang out in the summer night. It felt incongruous, that mirth, set against the undercurrent of tension humming through the quiet house.

On the opposite side of the room, Brian paced like a caged animal, arms folded tight across his chest. Every so often he paused at the window, craning his neck as if expecting to see something—anything—of value in the darkness outside. Roger couldn't blame him. It was easier to focus on something external than the helpless worry pressing down on them both. It felt as if they'd waited for hours. Was it normal for a birth to take this long?

He scrubbed a hand through his hair, fingers catching in the waves at the back of his neck. He'd never felt so useless. Brush and canvas he could command. A crisis of light or color he could fix with a careful stroke. But this? This long waiting, this not knowing … it was unbearable. And he wasn't even the expectant father.

From the barn, the strains of another waltz rose. He closed his eyes briefly, remembering Victoria in his arms, the sway of her skirt brushing his leg, her breath near his cheek. He would give anything to be dancing with her now, if only to see her smile, to feel the comfort of her nearness. He'd wanted to dance with her again, to keep on holding her. He would have done so . . . if not for the baby who'd decided to be born this night.

A sharp cry, distant and muffled, drifted down from upstairs. Brian froze mid-step. Roger stood.

Then—silence. Long and heavy. The clock ticked again.

Roger exhaled, a low, shaky breath. *Lord, let them be all right. Please.*

As if in answer to his prayer, another sound—thin, reedy at first, then rising strong and sure—pierced the stillness. A baby's cry.

For a breathless moment longer, Roger and Brian stood frozen, eyes locking across the room. Then Brian bolted for the stairs, taking them two at a time. Roger followed him, the pounding of their boots on the steps echoing through the house, chasing away the hush that had held it captive.

Brian threw open the bedroom door and entered, but Roger stopped at the threshold. Inside, lamplight bathed the room in a warm glow, golden and soft. Kit lay propped against a mound of pillows, her cheeks flushed, damp tendrils of hair clinging to her forehead. Cradled in her arms was a tiny bundle—the baby's face barely visible, but unmistakably new. Fragile. Perfect.

"We have a son," Kit said, her voice filled with wonder.

Brian sank to his knees at the side of the bed and reached out to touch both his wife and child. Kit smiled at him through tears.

Roger's gaze shifted. Victoria stood a little apart, near the corner of the room, as if reluctant to intrude on the family's private joy. Her hands were clasped at her waist, and her eyes shone with a reverent light. She looked different—still herself, still composed and beautiful but softer somehow. She'd witnessed a miracle, and it had marked her. He'd always admired her spirit, her courage, her strength. But this . . . this stillness, this reverence in her eyes … It humbled him. Moved him.

And in that instant, he knew—more certainly than ever before—that he wished to build something with this woman. To witness life with her. To see its sorrows and triumphs, its pain and its beauty together.

But should he want that life? Would it be fair to her? He'd given up the security of the thriving concern of Bernhardt & Son in London. He'd left his homeland to pursue his art in America. He'd promised to give himself whatever time was needed to perfect his craft. He'd planned to continue wandering the West, painting and drawing whatever caught his fancy. For now, he was homeless and didn't care. But what kind of life would that be for a woman? And even he didn't have to ask what type of life that would be for a child. It would be no life at all. Children needed a place to call home and the stability that came with roots, and he wasn't able to offer those to anyone.

He turned and made his way back down the stairs.

Chapter Nineteen

The first hint of morning pressed soft and silver against the windowpanes, though the sun itself had yet to rise. The lamp on the nightstand cast a pool of gold upon the floorboards and onto the rocking chair where Victoria sat, cradling the bundle of flannel and new life against her chest.

"Good morning, Grayson," she whispered.

Her nephew stirred slightly, his tiny mouth opening and closing. She gently adjusted the blanket and hummed a lullaby she half-remembered from childhood, the notes fragile on her lips. His head fit neatly in the crook of her arm, his features so impossibly small and perfect. Carved by heaven's own breath, it seemed.

She stole a glance toward the bed. Kit lay sleeping, one hand curled instinctively where the baby had rested beside her not long before. She looked young and pale but peaceful. The hard labor had taken its toll, but joy had followed in its wake.

Victoria rocked slowly, the chair creaking a quiet

rhythm into the still room. Her heart was filled to the brim in a way she hadn't expected. She hadn't done much—only held Kit's hand, fetched towels, whispered words of encouragement when Kit had cried out—but she'd been witness to a miracle. She had never seen anything like it. Never felt anything like it.

Grayson pulled a tiny arm free of his binding, making soft mewling sounds. A knot rose in her throat.

Boston felt a lifetime away. Its cobbled streets and well-ordered drawing rooms, the crisp rustle of newspapers, and the pale blue of her small bedroom seemed to belong to another person entirely. She had come west to find her brother. She had told herself it was temporary. Just a season. But now . . .

Now she couldn't imagine walking away from here. She wanted to be near Brian and his little family. Not just through letters or the occasional visit—if one could even be afforded. No, she wanted to be a part of their lives. And more specifically, of little Grayson's life. She wanted to celebrate his first tooth, his first steps, his first word.

She blinked quickly and pressed her lips to the baby's soft hair, breathing in the smell of him. "You've captured my heart, little one. How did that happen so quickly?"

The truth settled over her like a quilt pulled up to the chin. She couldn't leave. She *wouldn't* leave.

She didn't yet know how she would make a life in this place. She couldn't stay forever at Eden's Gate. William was kind, but she couldn't let herself impose upon him forever. She must find a way to earn a living.

But what could she do? She knew how to knit and sew. She could embroider delicate handkerchiefs and Bible verses to frame and hang on the wall. But what use was that?

"How long have you been holding him?" Kit asked in a gravelly voice, breaking into her reverie.

Victoria raised her eyes from the baby. "Not long. I looked in and saw him stirring. I didn't want him to wake you. You were sleeping so peacefully."

Kit smiled as her eyes drifted closed again. "Hmm. Thank you. It was good to sleep. It's more exhausting to give birth than I expected."

Perhaps Grayson already recognized his mother's voice, for his soft mewling turned to whimpers that held a note of urgency and promised to get louder quite soon.

Kit opened her eyes a second time as she pushed herself upright in the bed, her back braced with pillows. "He sounds hungry. I'd better try nursing him again."

Victoria rose from the rocking chair. "It'll be daylight soon." She placed the baby in Kit's waiting arms. "I imagine Brian will be back from the Hasting Ranch with your things before the sun is above the mountains."

"He's had an even longer night than I have."

"I'm not certain I would agree with that." She folded the blanket that had covered her lap and placed it on the rocking chair.

The door to the bedroom creaked softly as it opened, and Mrs. Adler stepped inside. Her gaze took in the bed and Victoria standing beside it. She gave

Victoria a nod before looking at Kit again. "Did you sleep well, Mrs. Townsend?"

"Yes, thank you." Kit stroked the baby's head with a finger, watching him as he suckled.

"Are you ready for something to eat yourself? I can bring you a tray."

"Oh, yes, please. I'm *starving*."

Victoria chuckled. "I will leave you then. I must get dressed and ready for the day."

"And you need to eat some breakfast yourself, Miss Castleton," the housekeeper called after her as Victoria slipped from the room.

Half an hour later—wearing a simple white blouse and navy blue skirt, her hair captured in a bun at the nape—Victoria entered the dining room. William and Roger were already there. She wondered if either of them had gotten more sleep than she had. William rose from the table and pulled out the chair for her.

"Will you be going into town for church?" he asked.

"No. I shall be satisfied with reading my Bible today. I want to be nearby, in case Kit needs anything."

"Of course you do." William settled onto his own chair again.

"It was quite a night, I daresay." Roger held out a platter of toasted bread in her direction.

"Yes, quite a night."

"And mother and baby are doing well?"

She nodded.

"Good. That's good."

She narrowed her eyes. He didn't seem himself this morning. He sounded stiff and formal. Why was that?

She remembered the waltz they'd shared the evening before, the way he'd held her in his arms, the way he'd looked at her with such tenderness, the resonant sound of his voice when he'd said, "One more dance?" She also remembered the way he'd disappeared so quickly from the doorway after the baby was born. Without a word to her or anyone else. Without hardly a glance in her direction.

She hadn't wondered about it then, but she wondered now. Which was silly, since she had much more important matters to think upon.

BREAKFAST WAS OVER and Roger had left the dining room by the time Brian arrived back at Eden's Gate, his arms holding everything he'd thought his wife and son might need over the next few days.

"Brian," Victoria said as he moved toward the staircase, "I would like a moment to speak with you. Not now. I know you're eager to be with Kit and Grayson. But later this morning. Perhaps when they are both sleeping again?"

"Sure. Of course. I'll look for you, Vicky."

She watched him climb the stairs and disappear into the bedroom.

"Something wrong?" William asked.

She turned to face him. "Not wrong, exactly." She considered for a moment. "But maybe it would be even better to talk to you."

One of his eyebrows arched in question as he motioned toward the parlor settee. "I'm all ears."

Victoria sat and waited for him to do the same. Then she said, "I've decided not to return to Boston. I'm going to stay in Gibeon."

Now his eyes widened. "That's quite a decision, Victoria."

"But not a bad one."

"No, not a bad one. I've simply never heard you express any desire to remain in the area."

She folded her hands in her lap. "It was always my intention to go home. But I . . . I've come to realize that Boston isn't home any longer. Home is here, near Brian and his family. But I . . . but there's a problem."

"What's that?"

"I will have to sell the house in Boston, of course. That will provide me with some money to live on. Of course, half of whatever the sale realizes will belong to Brian, but the rest should see me through for a time. It will allow me to rent a room in Gibeon or perhaps even a small house. However, I will still need to find employment. You know Gibeon so much better than I. Do you know who might be willing to hire me? I can sew and knit. I can clean. I am not a good cook, but I could work as a secretary. I have quite fine penmanship and am able to take notes quickly. I'm willing to learn."

His brows drew together in thought. "I don't know of anything right off. Nancy Davidson has a dress shop. She might need a seamstress. Fred Mason's an attorney. It's possible he might want a secretary, although I can't say he has a great deal of business. I'm not sure what else there might be. Let me think on it a spell. And please know that you may remain at Eden's Gate for as long as you like or need. Don't think your decision means you must hurry to leave the ranch. You are always welcome here."

Eyes watering, she looked down at her hands while blinking the tears away. "Thank you."

"Don't you worry." He stood. "We'll figure this out."

ALONE IN THE BUGGY, Roger let the horse choose its own speed on the return trip from Gibeon. Much of that morning's worship service had been lost on him. His thoughts had strayed to Eden's Gate time and again—and to the decision he knew he should make. He should finish the last of the commissioned paintings, ship them off to Rhode Island, and then leave. He should go on his way. To Oregon or California or wherever his fancy took him next.

It's what he *should* do.

Would he?

Roger couldn't recall a time when his emotions had been pulled in two opposing directions the way they were now. He'd had to wrestle with decisions before, of course, but his emotions had been set on one side or the other. Most times, it had been a battle between his heart and his head. This was different. His heart wanted to stay, and his heart wanted to leave. Both at the same time. His heart wanted to be with Victoria, and his heart told him he needed to be on his own.

"The heart is deceitful above all things, and desperately wicked: who can know it?"

The familiar Bible verse replayed in his head. His father had quoted it often as a warning when Roger was a boy.

"So . . ." He looked up at the sky, at the same time tapping the reins against the horse's rump. "If I can't trust my heart, how can I know what I should do?"

He heard no answer. Not that he expected to hear God's voice speaking from the expanse of blue. Although that might have made his life easier, if more than a little terrifying.

When he drove the buggy into the barnyard fifteen minutes later, his confusion hadn't lifted. He was glad to see William in the barn, mucking out a stall. As soon as he'd freed the buggy horse from its harness and traces and led it to the nearby corral, he went into the barn himself.

William rested a hand upon the pitchfork. "How was church?"

"Reverend Blankenship always preaches a good message. How are things here?"

"Quiet. Brian, Kit, and the baby are all in the upstairs bedroom, last time I was inside. Sleeping would be my guess. Mrs. Adler went to her own room to rest, and not long ago, Victoria told me she was going for a walk." He gestured toward the creek in the distance. "I told her it was too hot, but she's got lots on her mind."

"She does?"

"She's decided not to go back to Boston."

Roger took a step backward. "She's what?"

"She's going to stay in Idaho. In Gibeon. She wants to be close to her brother and his family. Plans to sell the house in Boston and settle here."

"When did she decide all that?"

"During the night, I guess. Told me about it after breakfast and asked for my help finding employment. You'd left the table by that time, and I didn't see you again before you left for Gibeon or I would've mentioned it."

Roger hadn't minded going alone to church. Between the barn dance and the birth of the baby the previous night, most of the residents and employees of Eden's Gate had good reasons to remain behind. Exhaustion chief amongst them. The solitary drive, both to and from town, had seemed a perfect time for Roger to reflect on just when, exactly, he meant to move on from the ranch. But suddenly he regretted going into Gibeon. If he hadn't gone to church alone, he might have been present when Victoria confided her decision to William. Better yet, she might have confided in him instead.

He took another step back from the stall. "Maybe I should check on her."

The right side of William's mouth quirked, but he said nothing. Simply nodded before lifting the pitchfork and returning to work.

Roger left the barn and strode in the direction of the creek, turning left to follow it toward the mountain range, the sun hot upon his head and back. The creek didn't rush and tumble as it had in the spring. Now it ran low. More than a trickle but not much more.

At last, he saw Victoria ahead of him, seated in the shade of a cottonwood tree, her back leaning against the trunk, her knees drawn up to her chest beneath her skirt. If she noticed his approach, she didn't let on. By her expression, she was lost in thought.

He stopped while he was still several yards away. "Miss Castleton."

She didn't seem to hear him.

"Victoria."

She looked in his direction, unseeing at first. Then her vision seemed to clear, and her eyes focused on him. "Mr. Bernhardt." She moved as if to rise.

"Don't get up." He closed the distance between them. "Please. Allow me to join you."

She relaxed against the tree trunk once again.

He sat beside her. After a moment or two, he removed his hat and set it on the ground before raking his fingers through his hair.

"I didn't realize the time," she said. "You're back from church already."

He acknowledged her words with a soft sound in his throat.

"Reverend Blankenship must think ill of us."

"The service was rather sparsely attended, and it wasn't just folks from Eden's Gate who were missing. Plenty of others decided to stay home too. Still worn out after all that dancing."

She smiled weakly. "I don't even know when people went home."

"It was late. Quite late." He turned his head to look

toward the Tetons. "William told me you've decided to remain in Idaho."

A pause, then, "Yes. I will sell the house in Boston and find a place to live in Gibeon. I'll take whatever work I can find. I want to be near Brian, Kit, and the baby."

"Of course you do. But that's quite a change of plans."

"Yes."

There was so much he wished he could say. He could have told her how he admired her. In the weeks since he'd met her on the road to the Yellowstone Lake Hotel, he'd learned that she was a woman who preferred order and routine. Yet she'd embarked on a search into the unknown, looking for her brother. And here she was, ready to embrace another drastic change. Change that would surely come with more than a little chaos and a great deal of the unknown. That took courage. More courage than she realized she possessed.

Perhaps he would have said all that to her. But before he could, she pushed to her feet.

"We should go back," she said. "Mrs. Adler will be serving Sunday dinner before long. We don't want her wondering where we are."

The moment to speak had come and gone. He stood and together they walked back to the house.

Chapter Twenty

Three days later, Brian drew the Overstreet buggy to a halt outside the Gibeon Telegraph Office, a narrow building sandwiched between the Drummond Brothers Bank and the Gibeon Weekly Times. As he looped the reins around the whip holder, he looked at Victoria. "You sure you want to do this?"

Mouth dry, she nodded. "I'm sure." She hated the reed-thin sound of her voice.

"All right then." Her brother stepped down from the buggy, then rounded the vehicle to help her do the same.

Victoria had written out the message that would go to the attorney, Marcus Peterman, who had settled their parents' estate years ago. She trusted him, although to be fair, he was the only lawyer she knew. Still, she would put the selling of the home and furniture in Boston into his hands and rely on him to see that her personal belongings were shipped west as soon as possible.

The bell above the door gave a sharp jangle as Victoria stepped into the telegraph office, Brian close behind her. The space swallowed her at once, narrow as a boxcar and barely wide enough for the two of them to stand abreast. A counter ran the length of the left wall, tall and worn, its edge rubbed smooth by years of elbows and ink-stained fingers. The room smelled of machine oil, old paper, and something faintly metallic, like the tang of a struck match.

It was stifling inside on this mid-August afternoon. The only window—a single pane of smudged glass fronting the street—let in a blade of light that stretched across the plank floor without reaching the counter that separated customers from the work area. Dust swirled in its path. The walls, painted a dull shade of green that had long ago surrendered to the smoke of lamps and wood stove, leaned inward ever so slightly. Victoria's breath caught at the sensation of being pressed in from all sides.

"Close in here, isn't it?" Brian muttered under his breath, shifting his shoulders as if to make more room for himself.

Caroline Drummond came out of the back room, her expression cool and unreadable. She was a slight woman with an air that hinted at her superiority to whomever stood on the opposite side of the counter. Her spectacles sat low on her nose as she regarded them over the top of the wire frames. "Good morning." Her voice was as crisp as the starch in her collar. "How may I help you?"

Brian removed his hat. "We'd like to send a wire."

Caroline nodded once, dipped her pen in an inkwell, and drew a blank form closer. The scratching of pen against paper filled the silence, punctuated by the steady ticking of the telegraph sounder on the desk behind her —a quiet, persistent code that seemed to echo off the close-set walls.

Victoria shifted closer to her brother, her arm brushing his. She'd never liked small spaces, but there was something about this one that felt particularly airless, as though the walls remembered every secret that had passed between them and refused to let even one escape.

Caroline looked up again. "What would you like the message to say?"

"I've written it out already." She placed the slip of paper on the counter and slid it toward the other woman.

TO: MARCUS PETERMAN, ATTORNEY, BOSTON, MASS.

FROM: VICTORIA CASTLETON, GIBEON, IDAHO

INSTRUCTED TO SELL HOUSE AND FURNISHINGS IMMEDIATELY STOP SHIP PERSONAL EFFECTS TO GIBEON IDAHO STOP RELYING ON YOUR DISCRETION STOP WILL WRITE DETAILS STOP GRATITUDE AND TRUST REMAIN UNCHANGED

The other woman perused the message, then looked up again. "Shall I mark it urgent?"

"Yes, please."

Caroline nodded and turned to the telegraph key, her fingers nimble as she began to tap out the message. The rhythmic clicks filled the narrow room—sharp, staccato bursts like rain on a metal roof. The air seemed even heavier now, as though the message itself was taking up space.

Had she made a mistake? Should she have returned to Boston? Had she prayed about this decision enough? Did Brian and Kit even want her to stay? She wanted to be near them but perhaps they didn't feel the same. Perhaps her brother had wanted to escape her for good. Perhaps he'd only pretended to be glad to see her.

Her heart pounded a rapid beat and the walls seemed to grow even closer.

Caroline faced them again, brushing a strand of hair from her temple. "The message is on its way. I will send word to Eden's Gate when I receive a reply."

"How much do I owe you?"

Caroline did a quick count of the words in the message. "That'll be fifty-four cents."

Victoria opened her reticule and placed the needed coins on the counter.

Caroline slid the money to the edge of the counter, allowing the coins to drop into her free hand. Then she gave an abrupt nod, turned, and without a word of farewell, disappeared into the back room.

Victoria exchanged a glance with her brother before they left the office.

"Now what?" Brian asked.

"I would like to get a few things at the mercantile. Then we can head back."

They got into the buggy, and Brian drove the horse the short distance to the Teton General Store.

Unlike the telegraph office, the mercantile felt open, even spacious, sunlight pouring through the windows that looked out on the main street of town. And unlike Caroline Drummond, Margaret Hathaway welcomed Victoria to the store with a broad smile and kind words.

"It's so good to see you, Miss Castleton. How is that precious nephew of yours? Oh, Mr. Townsend. I didn't see you there. Congratulations on the birth of your son."

"Thank you," Victoria and Brian replied in unison.

"I trust you are all doing well. What a surprise for the baby to be born on the night of the barn dance. Made for a memorable night, even if most of us didn't hear about it until later."

"Very true," Brian said.

Margaret's gaze focused on Victoria once again. "And I hear tell that you're going to stay in Idaho."

How on earth had Margaret Hathaway heard that news already? They'd only sent the telegram minutes ago, and there'd been no one else in the telegraph office at the time.

"Yes," she answered. "I'm going to stay."

"Well, I think it's grand." She placed her hands on her hips. "But here I stand, jawing. What can I do for you?"

ROGER STOOD BACK from the large canvas, a brush poised in one hand, his palette balanced in the other. The painting of a bison was nearly finished. It had taken shape stroke by painstaking stroke over the past few days. There was something about the massive beast that stirred his soul as its gaze met his. The painting didn't portray just an animal, he'd realized as he worked. It portrayed history, survival, the spirit of an untamed land, and he was determined to do it justice.

He'd begun with a foundation of raw umber and burnt sienna, sketching the heavy form of the creature with loose, gestural lines. Layer by layer, he'd built up the body, using yellow ochre and Venetian red to capture the warmer tones of the bison's thick hide, sunlit in places and shadowed in others. For the coarser, darker fur along the massive shoulders and forequarters, he'd mixed black with gray and touches of burnt umber, dabbing with a stiff hog-bristle brush to suggest the texture. He'd rendered the beast's curved horns with a careful blend of black, cold grey, and a whisper of white, giving them a chalky sheen like aged bone. The dark eyes—deep, reflective pools—he'd created with a mix of sepia and indigo, adding the faintest glimmer of white for light.

At his feet, crumpled rags bore evidence of trial and error, failed shadows, and over-bright highlights. But today the beast looked to him as though it might lift its shaggy head at any moment, huff a breath, and step out of the canvas.

Mrs. Kennedy would, he believed, be pleased with the results.

From the doorway of the guest cottage came William's voice. "Impressive."

Roger glanced over his shoulder. "I daresay. I believe I shall be proud of this one above all the others."

"You've got a right to be proud." William stepped inside, removing his hat as he did so. "God's blessed you with a great talent, my friend."

Days ago, Roger had pushed all of the parlor furniture to one side, turning the room into a studio where he could paint this, his most ambitious painting. One far too large to sit on his easel. Instead the stretched canvas and boards rested on two sawhorses.

"Looks almost too real for my blood." William moved to stand beside Roger. "As you'll remember, I had a close encounter with a cousin of this guy not long before you arrived on Eden's Gate."

"I do recall."

William rubbed his thigh in the spot where the buffalo's horn had speared him. "Wouldn't care to repeat it."

"And I wouldn't care to experience what happened to you even once." Roger motioned toward the pencil sketches of bison that he'd hung on the wall to his right. "I drew those from a healthy distance. I'll never forget seeing a stampeding herd in Yellowstone. I couldn't believe how fast they ran or how sharply they could change direction or how they jumped over obstacles." His gaze returned to the canvas. "This guy looks too large and ponderous to be agile, but I know that is not true."

"So, what's next when everything is done?"

"I've hired James Thurgood to build custom crates for shipping the paintings back east. This is the largest one and will take the most time to prepare for shipping. James will come out to the ranch next week so the canvases can be crated here. I won't have to transport them into town first."

"James is an excellent carpenter."

"Quite so. I saw some of his work while in town. Naturally, the crates don't have to be works of art themselves. They only have to protect what's inside."

William patted Roger's shoulder. "I'll let you get back to your work." He set his hat on his head as he turned to go. "Looks like Victoria and Brian are back from town." With that, he walked out of the cottage.

Roger had intended to resume work—he was so close to being finished—but knowing Victoria had returned from Gibeon drew him to the doorway instead. He watched as Brian helped her descend from the buggy. It was done then. She'd sent the telegram she'd talked about at breakfast. She was selling her home in Boston. She was staying in Idaho for good.

A strange feeling washed over him. A longing for something. Or perhaps it was envy he felt. But that couldn't be it. Why would he be envious of Victoria? He didn't want to stay in one place. Despite his feelings for her, he didn't want to put down roots. He'd fought against that very thing for much of his adult life. Why would he envy Victoria's decision to settle here? No, that wasn't what he felt. It couldn't be.

He faced the painting of the great American bison once again. In a matter of weeks, this canvas could be framed and on display in the Whitaker Gallery in Providence, Rhode Island. And if it pleased Susannah Kennedy and Algernon Whitaker, in a matter of additional weeks, there could be other patrons of the arts demanding his work. He'd scarcely had the courage to hope that many people might see and admire his art. But now? Now it seemed possible. It was within his reach. Even his father might have been proud of him.

Why then did that strange, unwelcome feeling linger?

Chapter Twenty-One

Victoria held the baby—all of six days old—close to her chest as she carried him toward the buggy, the morning sun riding the crest of the Tetons. She waited until Kit settled onto the seat before passing the sleeping infant into her waiting arms.

"You come down to see us," Kit said.

"I will."

Brian pulled her into a warm embrace. "Make it soon."

"I will," she repeated, her throat thick with emotion.

As Brian got into the buggy, Victoria stepped back from it, fighting a wave of tears. She forced a smile and waved until the buggy—and the little family in it—disappeared from view. Her smile disappeared at once, and sadness threatened to swamp her. Silly, really. It wasn't as if she were alone. And it wasn't as if she wouldn't see them all again. It would have been so much worse had she been bidding them farewell before going back to Boston. So much worse.

She took a deep breath.

There. That was better.

She started toward the house, then stopped when she saw Roger in the open doorway of the main house.

"They're gone then," he said.

Both William and Roger had said goodbye to Brian and Kit at breakfast. After the meal, the two men had slipped away, giving Victoria time to be alone with her family. She was grateful for their thoughtfulness. Now she was grateful that Roger hadn't stayed hidden. His presence made her feel better.

"They're gone," she echoed.

"It's been quite a week."

"Yes."

By mutual but unspoken agreement, they moved toward two chairs on the porch. Once settled, they both looked toward the Tetons, now bathed in full light.

"I've always loved the sea," Victoria said softly, "and I shall miss being close to it. But I do believe, in the short time I've been here, that I've come to love those mountains even more."

"They are as magnificent, I daresay, as any that can be found in the world."

"You have painted them often, have you not?"

"I have. At many different hours of the day. From sunrise to sunset."

"Tell me what it is you see."

"What I see?"

"Yes, when you look at those mountains throughout the day. Describe to me what you see. Please."

He was silent a long while. She waited patiently,

somehow knowing he would do his best to satisfy her request.

At long last, he began, "The Tetons rise like a cathedral against the eastern sky. Severe, breathtaking, and ever-changing beneath the light of the day. At dawn, they are shadowed and still, their jagged edges inked in black against the paling sky. As the sun climbs up behind them, the peaks are nothing but silhouettes, sharp and solemn, but then, as the sun crests the range, light spills over their eastern faces and begins to reach this side, gilding the highest tips first. A pale halo forms around the summits, and the darkness softens into hues of periwinkle and lavender. Soon after, the peaks blush faintly, delicate pink and peach, as if the stones themselves have flushed under the touch of morning."

She had watched the sunrise from this porch more than once in the weeks she'd been on Eden's Gate, and his words captured what she'd witnessed to perfection. Her heart sang in response to his words.

"By midday," he said, his voice growing stronger, "with the sun overhead, the mountains grow bolder. The light pours directly onto the western slopes, revealing every granite crease and snowfield. Their colors flatten somewhat—cool steel grays and quiet slate blues—but their textures come alive. You can see the depth of every crevice, the dance of shadow and sun across the rock. They appear as they are. Immovable. Timeless."

Immovable and timeless. He was so right. Those mountains would still stand long after Victoria Castleton was in the grave. For some reason, that thought made her feel grounded and safe.

"You can see them soften again in late afternoon. As the sun lowers behind this house, its rays stretch low and warm across the valley, striking the Tetons full-on. That's when they turn golden—truly golden—bathed in amber light that clings to every ridge and spire. Dust in the air catches the light too, turning the space between us and the mountains into a veil of honey. It is brief, that moment, but it is there. As shadows grow long across the valley floor, the whole range seems to exhale, as if settling in for the night."

"Mr. Bernhardt." She was tempted to reach over and touch his arm but resisted the impulse. "I believe you have the soul of a poet."

He chuckled before continuing, his voice now resonant, like the scene he described. "It is just before dusk, when the sun has nearly set, that the Tetons take on their final hues. I think this might be my favorite time of all. Perhaps because it is fleeting and so difficult to capture with my paints. The light fades from the mountains' flanks, and the sky behind them deepens into mauve and violet, framing them in majesty. The granite grows blue-gray again, touched at the edges with a lingering pink. Little by little, the mountains return to silhouette, just as they were at dawn."

She tore her gaze from the mountains to look at Roger instead. Yes, he definitely had the soul of a poet. Perhaps that was what allowed him to create his beautiful paintings. He could put words to the things in the world that she could see, perhaps even feel, but couldn't describe. Her thoughts were earthbound while his were not.

He met her gaze, and her breath caught in her chest as she imagined him leaning forward to brush his lips against hers.

Such foolishness. Perhaps her thoughts weren't as earthbound as she'd once believed.

———

ROGER WAS NOT A POET, no matter what Victoria said. He had simply described what he'd seen and what he'd tried to capture in his many paintings since his arrival on Eden's Gate. And yet, as he found himself starting to drown in the hazel pools of her eyes, he longed to be exactly the man she thought him to be.

"Roger," she mouthed.

His pulse quickened in response.

The clip-clop of horse's hooves stopped him from doing something undoubtedly reckless, imprudent, and unfair. To himself as well as to Victoria. He broke his gaze from hers and turned in time to see Truman Blankenship arrive in the barnyard. He stood and stepped to the railing, watching as the reverend got out of his buggy.

The reverend smiled when he noticed Roger on the porch. "Good morning, Mr. Bernhardt." He gave a small wave. "And you, Miss Castleton."

"Good morning," Roger answered. "What brings you out this way?"

"I actually needed to speak with Miss Castleton."

Victoria stood beside Roger now. "To me?"

"Yes." The reverend continued to smile as he walked toward them. "How are Mrs. Townsend and the baby?"

"They are well. In fact, they are on their way back to the Hasting Ranch even now." She motioned toward the chairs on the porch. "Would you like to join us here or would you prefer to go into the parlor?"

"Here is good. It's a fine morning, although it will be hot soon enough."

The reverend waited until Victoria sat again. Then he took a seat.

Roger looked between them before asking, "If this is a private conversation, I can make myself scarce."

Victoria gave the reverend a questioning look.

It was Truman who answered, "It is not private."

Rather than sitting with them, Roger leaned his back against a post, offering them a whisper of privacy even though he was still present.

The reverend cleared his throat. "I'll get straight to it then. We've come upon a bit of a problem in Gibeon. Our schoolteacher, Mr. Corbin, received news two days ago that his sister in Salt Lake City has taken ill. Seriously ill. He left this morning to care for her and he says he will be unable to return."

"I am sorry to hear that. It must be difficult for him."

"It is. And it leaves us in a bind. School begins in just over two weeks. The board met last night, and your name came up."

"My name?" Victoria glanced at Roger, then back to the man in the nearby chair.

Reverend Blankenship nodded. "Several of our

board members—Mrs. Hathaway in particular—have spoken highly of you. And it was your brother who told me how much you value a good education. You've made an impression, Miss Castleton."

"I? But I have no experience. And certainly I have no teaching certificate."

The reverend smiled. "No one expects you to know everything at once. As for the certificate, the law allows for temporary appointments in cases like this. You could begin under provisional terms and take the certification exam later. The superintendent's a reasonable man. If you're willing, I believe he'll support the arrangement."

Victoria seemed stunned. "I . . . I don't know what to say."

"The position comes with a small house for you to live in and a modest salary."

She looked at Roger again, this time her gaze lingering. "What do you think?"

What did he think? He thought she was perfect. He thought she would settle in Gibeon and become an integral part of the community. He thought she would enchant the children and their parents alike. He thought every single male within twenty or thirty miles would find plenty of reasons to ride into Gibeon in the hope of meeting her, courting her. He thought—

"Mr. Bernhardt?"

He smiled instead of grinding his teeth. "Victoria, I believe God has answered your prayers in record time. You need a job and you want a home in Gibeon. Now you've been offered both."

"Amen to that." The reverend stood and placed his

hat on his head. "You pray about it. You can give me your answer when you come to church on Sunday. If you decide to take the job, we'll make arrangements from there. But I'll need to hear from you by then. No later. As I said, it isn't long before school starts, and we must have a teacher. If you decline, we must seek elsewhere." He bid them both farewell before returning to his buggy. Within minutes he'd disappeared from view, gone as quickly as he'd come.

"A teacher," Victoria said softly, wonder in her voice. "Even when our circumstances changed so dramatically when I was a child, my mother was determined her offspring would receive a sound education. I loved learning as a girl, and Mother made certain my schooling was as thorough as Grayson's. Do you suppose I can make the children in Gibeon love learning as much as I loved it?"

"I think you can do whatever you set your mind to, Miss Castleton."

In a strange way, he wished that wasn't true.

Chapter Twenty-Two

Roger wasn't surprised when Victoria told Reverend Blankenship that she would take the teaching position. And he enjoyed the pleasure he heard in her voice when Margaret Hathaway took her to see the small house nestled in a copse of trees behind the school. It wasn't much to look at: clapboard walls faded to a silvery gray, a shingled roof bowed slightly at the center, and a front step that creaked under Margaret's sure tread. But based on Victoria's reaction, he would have thought it second only to a palace.

"It's charming!" She clapped her hands in front of her lips. Then she looked at Roger and William who waited a few steps behind her. "I cannot believe this is happening."

"Believe it, Miss Castleton." Margaret opened the door to the house, then motioned for Victoria to enter first. "Mr. Corbin is a bachelor, and he took everything that was his when he left Gibeon. Whatever you see inside has been provided for your use."

Roger hung back, letting the women step inside first. He glanced at William, who offered a faint smile and a small shrug, then followed them in.

The interior smelled faintly of pine, old books, and wood smoke. It was a single room to start—an open sitting and cooking area with a black cast-iron stove, a narrow counter with basin and pump, and a scarred wooden table with two mismatched chairs. A colorful braided rug, faded by time, softened the floor near the hearth. Light streamed through gingham-curtained windows, casting gentle shadows over everything.

The furnishings were modest, yes, but cared for. A small bookshelf stood against one wall, with several readers and arithmetic primers lining the top shelf beside a Bible and a ceramic vase filled with dried flowers. On the far side of the room, a door stood ajar, revealing a glimpse of the narrow bedroom—a bed with a patchwork quilt, a washstand, and a simple pine dresser.

He watched Victoria as her gloved fingers brushed lightly over the back of a chair. She said nothing as she turned slowly, taking it all in. Then she looked at Margaret. "It's more than charming. It's perfect. Truly. Thank you."

Roger felt something shift in his chest, not unlike the sensation he got when he stood before a blank canvas and knew, suddenly, what the first stroke must be. She meant it. She saw what this place could mean for her. It wasn't just a roof and walls, but a new beginning.

Margaret began listing items that could be brought over from the mercantile—a kettle, fresh linens, maybe a curtain rod for the bedroom. Roger only half-listened. He continued to watch Victoria, noting how she turned a second time, pleasure in her eyes.

When her gaze met his, she offered a smile. "I think I shall be happy here."

And Roger, standing in the doorway with one hand braced against the frame, thought to himself that he would paint this moment if he could—the sunlight, the softness in her voice, the courage behind her words. He would paint it not because it was grand, but because it was true.

Margaret held out a key tied onto a worn strip of leather. "This is yours."

Victoria took it.

"You should plan to move in by next Saturday. You will have much to prepare before the opening day of school."

Victoria looked at William, a question in her eyes.

"Don't worry," he answered. "We'll bring you to town whatever day you wish."

She nodded and returned her gaze to Margaret. "Then I shall move in a few days."

"Good. That's good. You come see me at the store if you find you need anything."

"I will."

Margaret bid them all a good day and left the house.

"It's all happened so fast," Victoria said softly.

Roger was fairly certain she wasn't aware she'd spoken the words aloud. The look of happiness she'd worn a short while before had been replaced by one of uncertainty. It tugged at his heart. Made him want to encourage her, comfort her.

But she was right about one thing. It had all happened fast. She would move from Eden's Gate in a matter of days. Perhaps only two. Perhaps even tomorrow. It wouldn't take much to move her. She had little more than what would fit into the trunk and valise that had accompanied her across the country.

One thing he knew without doubt: The ranch would feel empty and lifeless without her there.

"Come on." William held out an arm. "Mrs. Adler's waiting for us with the carriage."

William and Victoria led the way out of the house. Roger took one last look around before following after them.

AFTER SUNDAY DINNER, Victoria went onto the Eden's Gate porch to read. With her stomach pleasantly full and the heavy warmth of the afternoon, she had to fight to keep her eyes focused on the page of her book. It was a battle she soon lost.

Music from a guitar and voices raised in song pulled her from her slumber. She straightened in the chair, rolling her head from side to side to loosen a kink in her neck. When she stood, she noticed her book, splayed open, on the porch floor. She took a moment to pick it up, checking to see that no pages had been damaged when it slid off her lap. Then she placed the book on the small, round table nearby before stepping to the railing and leaning forward to look around the corner of the house.

As they often did on a Sunday afternoon, several cowboys had gathered in the shade of the trees, not far from the back door. Logan Coe strummed his guitar as the men broke into a new song.

"What a fellowship, what a joy divine / Leaning on the everlasting arms / What a blessedness, what a peace is mine / Leaning on the everlasting arms." Softly, she added her voice to theirs as they began the chorus. "Leaning, leaning / Safe and secure from all alarms / Leaning, leaning / Leaning on the everlasting arms."

She straightened back from the porch railing, allowing the lyrics to take hold in her heart. It was as if God had tapped her on the shoulder and whispered, *My daughter, you are safe in My arms. You may have peace as you face the future.*

Strange, she hadn't known she needed reassurance until the reassurance came. Yes, she'd felt overwhelmed at times, especially when she considered her new position as teacher to the children of Gibeon. But understanding that God was with her as she embarked on this new adventure? It changed everything.

Movement off to her right drew her gaze in time to see Roger entering the guest cottage. Recently, it had become his art studio, and she was dying to see what he'd created over the past week or so. Soon she wouldn't be able to walk across the barnyard to see him, talk to him, look at his paintings. This would be one of her last chances to do so.

She obeyed the tug on her heart and left the porch,

making her way toward the guest cottage. The door was open, and she stopped just inside the threshold, her breath catching when her gaze fell on the enormous painting leaning against the opposite wall. The American bison stood solitary and immense on the canvas, emerging from a sweep of golden grass and distant haze, its shaggy coat rendered with such depth she fancied she would feel the rough texture of its fur were she to touch it.

Roger appeared from the connecting bedroom and stopped when he saw her.

"It looks so real," she said.

A smile tugged at the corners of his mouth. "Thank you."

"It's almost frightening it's so real. As if it charged out of the painting, and it would have to go through me to get outside."

He chuckled as he moved to stand beside her. "I've grown frightfully fond of the dear chap as I worked on him. All those long hours he and I have spent together in this room. But I assure you, he will do you no harm."

"Will you be sorry to part with the painting?"

"Perhaps a little. I can't help thinking it is one of the best things I've done since coming to America. I only hope Mrs. Kennedy will be pleased when she sees it. A painting of a buffalo was her one request."

Victoria stared at the canvas again. "She'll be pleased with it. It's spectacular."

"Spectacular, is it? If it weren't promised to the Whitaker Gallery, I do believe I would give it to you for your new home in Gibeon."

She turned a surprised gaze on him, about to say there wasn't one wall big enough in the teacher's house. Then she caught sight of the teasing glint in his eyes. "Sir, you are ridiculous."

Their smiles blossomed at the same time.

"Miss Castleton, I fear you are not the first person to think me so. My father often said the same."

Despite his smile, his voice revealed a hint of pain. And it reminded her of her brother when she'd told Brian that his plans to go west were ridiculous. She'd meant to keep him from making a bad choice, and instead she'd wounded him. And now she understood that Roger had been wounded too.

"I'm sorry," she said quickly. "I didn't mean that. I meant . . . I knew you were teasing me. About the painting. It would never fit in that small house."

"Indeed."

Something new flickered in his blue eyes. Something that made her stomach flutter. She found it impossible to draw a breath. Was there no air left in the room, despite the open door behind her?

He shifted his body toward her. Instinctively, she did the same.

"Victoria."

Her name, whispered, caused the fluttering to erupt anew inside of her.

He placed his hands ever so lightly on her shoulders. His eyes searched hers as his head lowered, questioning her, allowing her time to stop what was about to happen.

She didn't stop it.

Victoria had never been kissed. Not by a man on the

lips. Not in the way Roger kissed her now. She was unprepared for the feelings that swept through her. The tingling of her lips. Those wretched, intoxicating, overwhelming, sickening, amazing flutters in her stomach. The loss of strength in her knees. If not for his hands slipping from her shoulders to her waist, she was certain she would have crumpled to the ground.

When he drew back—was it a moment since the kiss began or an eternity?—he whispered, "I should not have done that."

"Why?" The word was inaudible.

"Because it made me want to do it again."

Do it again! her mind shouted.

Perhaps he would have, but the sound of men's voices alerted them to the presence of others. His fingers gently squeezed her waist before his hands dropped away and he took one step back.

The small space between them felt like a chasm.

Chapter Twenty-Three

By the time James Thurgood arrived at Eden's Gate on Monday morning, Roger had removed all of the furniture—with the exception of the large bookcase —from the parlor of the guest cottage. While the building of the crates would take place outside, the final work would be done indoors, protecting the canvases from the heat and dust of the barnyard.

The first thing James did—after measuring the largest of the paintings—was set up sawhorses in the shade of the cottonwoods. Next he and Roger unloaded the pine boards, tools, and other supplies from the wagon bed. Before long, the rhythmic rasp of a hand saw filled the morning quiet.

Roger leaned a shoulder against a tree, arms folded, and watched James as he set aside the saw and took up the hand plane, sliding it along the edge of a board, each pass curling up a ribbon of pale wood that floated to the ground like a slip of paper. James worked without fuss or wasted motion, measuring and fitting the slats with practiced hands, his sleeves rolled past his elbows, sawdust clinging to the hair on his forearms. The scent of cut wood mingled with those of horse dung, hay, and wild sage.

"Won't be light," James said as he fit one side panel into place. "But it'll hold. Enough bracing here to see your painting safe to Rhode Island, and maybe back again if they're daft enough to return it."

Roger offered a half-smile as he pushed off the tree. "Let's hope they're not daft." He stepped closer, fingers trailing lightly along the sanded edge. Already he could picture the painting inside—the great bull buffalo, its eyes fixed forward with a look that was something between defiance and weariness.

"We'll carry it inside once the lid's ready." James wiped his brow with the back of his wrist.

Roger had plenty of padding awaiting the final stage —muslin to cover the surface of the canvas and straw and felt for the pressure points and corners. In addition, James had made shock-absorbing braces to keep the canvas and its frame from shifting inside the crate. The smaller paintings would be packaged with just as much care, but it was the almost life-sized one of the bison that meant the most to him. He wasn't sure why. He only knew it was true. He wished he could be there when the crate was opened and Mrs. Kennedy got her first glimpse of his dear, majestic chap.

Movement off to the side drew his gaze in time to see William striding toward him.

When his friend reached his side, he asked, "Will your paintings be ready to ship by this afternoon?"

"I think so. Why?"

"I thought we could kill two birds with one stone. I'm moving Miss Castleton to Gibeon and thought we could haul your crates in the wagon at the same time."

"Will there be room?"

William chuckled. "You know yourself that she travels amazingly light for a woman. Just that one trunk and a valise. Plenty of room in the wagon bed. However, you'll want your horse, or you'll have to sit on her trunk behind the wagon seat."

Roger glanced toward the second story, although the bedrooms were on the opposite side of the house, their windows looking west. He wondered what Victoria was doing at this moment. Packing the last of her things into that trunk? Removing all signs that she'd slept in that bedroom for almost a month now? Talking with Mrs. Adler or Chuck? Probably the latter. Both the house-keeper and cook had come to love Victoria.

As have I.

His breath stuttered in his chest.

Yes, he loved her. No question about it. It wasn't simple affection he felt. It was love.

This was the first time he'd used the word, although he'd been aware of the growing emotion long before now. He simply hadn't acknowledged it.

He *loved* her.

He loved her and she was going away. It was better for her that she go. Better that she make a life in Gibeon where she could put down roots. He knew it. Wanted it for her sake. Because he didn't want roots. Not yet. Not now. Still . . .

William's hand alighted on Roger's shoulder. "Let me know if you and Mr. Thurgood need help with that crate." With that, he strode toward the barn, leaving Roger with his troubled thoughts.

THE SUN PRESSED down like a heavy hand, and dust of the road clung to Victoria's skin. Heat shimmered in waves across the dry landscape, and the only sounds were the rhythmic creak of the box wagon, the occasional snort from the team, and the faint clop of horses' hooves.

The bench seat was unforgiving, a plank of wood with no cushion and no backrest, and she found herself bracing with one hand against the rough edge to keep from sliding as the wagon jostled over another rise. Her other hand tightened around the folds of her skirt. Beside her, William held the reins with quiet confidence, squinting into the sunlight as the horses plodded onward.

Behind them, the wagon bed was filled to the brim. Her own modest trunk was tucked near the rear corner, along with her valise, a crate of books that William had presented her from his library, and some food stores Mrs. Adler had insisted she would need. But it was Roger's crated paintings that took up most of the space —wooden boxes carefully tied down, one of them massive, big enough that it stretched nearly the width of the wagon floor. With each small jolt of the wheels, she heard the creak of wood and rope. The crates had been padded with blankets and straw, but still ... Could a deep rut undo all that care?

Roger hadn't said much about the paintings as they'd prepared to leave Eden's Gate, only checked each crate one last time. But she'd seen the tension in his shoulders. She felt the same. Every bump and sway of the wagon reminded her of all that was being carried—Roger's work, her belongings, and something far less tangible: the life that waited for her at the end of the road. A one-room schoolhouse, a borrowed home tucked behind it, and a task she wasn't at all certain she was prepared for.

Did Roger feel as uncertain about the future as she did?

Another bounce of the wagon made her clutch the edge of the seat tighter, the sun glinting off the metal bracket below. She drew in a breath, but the air was heavy with heat and dust. She covered her mouth and coughed.

"We're almost there," William said.

She knew that, of course. She'd traveled this road often enough over the past weeks for it to be familiar to her. The town would soon be in sight. Still, her previous trips to and from Gibeon had been made in a surrey, a shaded vehicle built for comfort. The same could not be said of this wagon meant for transporting freight and ranch supplies. She could only pray her teeth wouldn't rattle out of her head before they arrived at their destination.

"We'll take you to your home first."

She met his gaze and nodded, the words repeating in her head. *My home. I have a new home.*

The thought did nothing to comfort her.

Minutes later, the wagon creaked to a halt beneath the cottonwoods that shaded the small teacher's house, the leaves unmoving in the breezeless heat. Victoria drew in a shallow breath and rose from the miserable bench. She was already on the ground by the time William looped the reins around the brake handle. She glanced at the house—the narrow porch, the morning glory vines winding around the posts, the tidy door with its iron latch. Unlike the first time she'd seen this house, she felt no surge of welcome, only the dull churn of apprehension rising again in her chest.

Roger dismounted and tied his horse alongside the team. He didn't speak, only moved to the back of the wagon and began unfastening the ropes. Then he lifted down her trunk and carried it up the porch steps. Victoria followed him to open the door. The little house was as she'd left it yesterday after church, quiet and still.

Next came William with her valise and the box of books. He set them both on the floor beside her trunk.

Mrs. Adler had told her what was in the final crate —jars of fruits and jams, biscuits, a loaf of bread. Nourishment. Comfort. The housekeeper's way of saying, *You're not alone.*

With the last of her belongings brought in, William tugged the brim of his hat and said, "We'll be on our way, then. Freight office closes soon."

Victoria nodded, then walked out onto the porch again. Roger went to the wagon and tied his saddle horse to the back of it. She longed for him to say something to her. Anything. When he didn't, she left the porch. "Roger."

The brim of his hat cast a shadow over his eyes when he looked back.

"Thank you for helping me today," she said, trying to keep her voice steady. "And for riding behind the wagon in this heat."

His mouth curved faintly. "Didn't trust William not to jolt the whole lot into the ditch."

She attempted to return his smile, but what she wanted was to ask what yesterday had meant—if that kiss had stirred something in him the way it had in her. But the question lodged in her throat. This wasn't the place for it, especially with William present. Besides, she didn't want to ask if she wasn't ready to hear his answer. Not if it wasn't the answer she wanted.

He gave her a nod that was too polite to be personal. "We'd better get to the freight office."

"Of course."

He hesitated, as if there were something more to say, then turned and climbed up to the wagon seat. In another moment, the wagon rumbled away from the house, the team plodding slow and steady, the remaining crates shifting slightly with the motion.

Victoria watched them go, remaining where she was until the wagon passed out of sight, dust curling in its wake, and the stillness folded around her again.

Chapter Twenty-Four

Roger stood outside the guest cottage, the sun high and merciless above him. His shirt clung to his back with sweat, and a bead rolled down from his temple, stinging his eye before he swiped it away. The door to the little house gaped open, the hinge creaking now and again like an old man complaining.

He hadn't painted anything since Victoria left Eden's Gate five days earlier.

He stepped into the cottage, beyond the reach of the relentless sun. The room smelled of pine wood and linseed oil, but the scents were fading. The furniture—sofa, chairs, table—had been returned to their proper places, and there was no hint of an artist's studio within these walls, with the exception of a few smudges of ochre and umber on the floorboards. His most recent paintings were gone—shipped off to Providence, where they'd be framed and studied by strangers with culti-vated tastes and cool expressions. At least that was his expectation.

While he had loved the days spent in this room painting the massive bison, it wasn't his work that filled his thoughts now. It was the memory of Victoria that washed over him—standing with him in this same space, his hands on her waist, his lips upon hers.

He had planned to leave Eden's Gate after his return from Yellowstone. But nothing had gone according to plan this summer. Not since his coach had stopped behind the stage with a busted wheel, and he'd offered a ride to the tall young woman with hazel eyes and dark brown hair.

He crossed to the window and pressed a hand against the frame, looking out across the land. Brown patches spread through the nearby pasture like spilled tea. The creek that cut through the Eden's Gate range was no more than a shallow ribbon as August waned. Even the cottonwoods looked weary, their leaves limp and dust-dulled.

Releasing a heavy breath, he turned and left the cottage. Spying William standing at the corral, he moved in his direction.

"Another hot day," William said without looking his way.

Roger stopped beside his friend and mirrored his position, arms resting on the top rail, one foot braced on the bottom rail.

"If we don't get rain soon, we're going to be in a bind. The grazing's poor. Might have to sell off some of the yearlings ahead of schedule. Prices won't be good, but better now than when everyone's desperate."

Roger nodded slowly, following the line of William's gaze. "It's hard to watch the land go thirsty."

They were quiet a long while after that.

Finally, William said, "Quiet around here this last week."

Roger didn't have to ask what he meant. "Do you think Victoria's doing all right?"

"The folks of Gibeon will have made sure she feels welcome."

"She's never taught school before. She was anxious about it. I could tell."

"You know what I think?"

"What?"

"You miss her."

Roger hesitated, then answered, "Don't you?"

"Of course I do." William chuckled. "But not for the same reason. Not in the same way."

"Am I so easy to read?"

"Not all the time. But when it comes to your feelings about Miss Castleton, you are pretty much an open book."

Roger turned his back to the corral fence and leaned against it, his gaze now on the main house. "I never meant to stay at Eden's Gate this long. First, I was supposed to go back to England. Then, after I sold Father's business, I planned to travel around America. Paint more places. Experience more of this country of yours."

"But now?"

He shook his head as he looked at his friend. "I do not know. What is there to keep me here?"

William arched a brow.

"How would I make a living? Unlike Sebastian, I am not meant to be a rancher or one of your ranch hands. I have no yearning to return to the drapery business. I'm an artist."

"An artist who got a commission for five paintings for a gallery in Providence."

"True. But one commission will not support me for long. And there is no guarantee of another."

William's gaze remained intent.

"The life of an artist is not a secure way of life. My father drummed that into me."

"Not secure for a wife, you mean?"

Is that what he'd meant? Yes, he supposed it was. He didn't mind the uncertainty for himself. He could live on surprisingly little. But a woman like Victoria would mind the uncertainty, the potential scarcity, a life without roots. Besides, she wanted to be near her brother. After all she'd been through to find him, she wouldn't want to traipse off into the great unknown with him. A future for the two of them wasn't possible.

William pushed off the corral railing. "Don't you suppose you should talk to her about it?"

Should he? He shrugged.

"Well, think about it." William tugged the brim of his hat before striding toward the house.

Roger suspected he would continue to think of little else.

VICTORIA SAT in the chair on the narrow front porch, grateful for the many trees that surrounded the little house, the leafy branches protecting it from the afternoon sun. Thankful she had some time with nothing new demanding her attention, she closed her eyes and listened to the sounds that drifted to her secluded location. A child's laughter and a mother's scolding reply. The clop of horses hooves and the creak of wagon wheels. The buzz of a fly. The rustle of underbrush caused by some small creature. A chipmunk perhaps. The bark of a dog from a distance.

The days since her move to Gibeon had passed in a blur of activity. She had settled into her little home. With only one trunk holding her belongings, it didn't take much time. After that, she'd tackled the schoolhouse, cleaning, arranging, acquainting herself with the readers, ordering supplies, making sure there was wood for the stove. The stifling heat of August made that latter task feel foolish, but summer would pass and winter would come. She didn't want to be caught unprepared.

On Wednesday, she'd met with several members of the school board and been apprised of the steps she must take to acquire her teacher's certification. She would have to pass exams administered in the courthouse in Saint Anthony, the county seat. Although the exams were normally offered only once a year, exceptions were made in an emergency. The lack of a teacher in Gibeon qualified as such. The testing would take a full day and include subjects such as reading and literature, orthography, penmanship, grammar and composition, arithmetic, geography, U.S. history and civics, physiology and hygiene, and pedagogy.

"We have textbooks that you can use to prepare," Margaret Hathaway had told her. "If you do not feel ready by October, we can ask for an extension until after the spring thaw. I know the superintendent. He will be patient with us."

The reverend added, "And I will be happy to help you review as often as you might like. Whenever you feel the need for assistance, I will make myself available."

She opened her eyes, her thoughts returning to the present.

Everyone she'd encountered in Gibeon had been kind and welcoming. Especially the parents of the children—ranging in age from six to fourteen—who would be her students. A representative from almost every family had stopped by to see her over the past few days, and the women had never failed to bring something for her. A loaf of sourdough bread. A half dozen eggs. Mason jars of preserved peaches and applesauce and pickled beets. A crock of freshly churned butter. A spice cake in a tin for her to keep. A bar of homemade soap scented with pine. A sachet of dried lavender for her dresser drawer.

In Boston, after her family's financial failure, Victoria had become estranged from those she'd thought were her friends. The move to a smaller home set amid other modest homes had made her feel isolated. That had only worsened after the death of her mother and stepfather.

But she wasn't isolated in Gibeon, and the realization warmed her heart.

A sound caught her attention. A sound quite out of place. A squeak? She straightened, listening. There it was again—a thin, pitiful little cry, coming from somewhere near the lilac bush that grew at the corner of the house. She rose and stepped down from the porch.

The dry grasses brushed against her skirts as she crouched beside the bush, gently pushing back the lower branches. A small bundle of orange-and-white fur sat tucked against the base of the shrub, wide eyes blinking up at her. The kitten's ribs showed through its thin coat, and one ear bore a jagged nick, as if it had gotten the worst of some encounter. But its meow was determined, even defiant, as though it had summoned her on purpose.

"Oh, you poor thing." She reached out slowly so as not to frighten it.

The kitten didn't move. Instead, it collapsed into her palm at the first touch, allowing her to draw it out of its hiding place and cradle it against her bodice.

"You're so thin. You must be starving." She stood and carried the kitten back to the porch, where she settled onto the chair again, still holding the small feline close. It began to purr—an uneven, sputtering sound that nevertheless melted her heart. "I haven't any cream, but I do have a bit of butter and a saucer of water. Perhaps I could boil a soft egg for you. Are you old enough to digest it?"

Holding the kitten between both hands, she held it

far enough away to see its belly, hind legs dangling. Then, smiling, she drew it back again.

"Well, little girl, you need a name." She stroked its bony spine.

It gave another tiny mew.

"Something brave and hopeful."

The kitten pressed its head beneath her chin and purred again.

She closed her eyes for a moment. "Hope. That's a good name. I'm going to call you Hope."

Chapter Twenty-Five

Before the congregation disbanded after the church service, Victoria was officially welcomed as Gibeon's new schoolteacher. She shook hands and said, "Thank you," time and time again before the sanctuary emptied of people. But finally, the last person headed home for Sunday dinner, leaving behind only Roger, William, and Victoria. They, along with Reverend Blankenship, had been invited to dine with the Hathaways. Mrs. Adler would have been included, but she had stayed at the ranch due to a cold.

As the group made their way to the Hathaway home—a two-story house connected to the general store through a doorway at the back of the mercantile—Roger fell into step beside Victoria. "You look well," he said after a brief silence.

"Thank you." She felt her cheeks grow warm at the compliment. But perhaps that was just the heat of the day.

"Have you settled in all right? Is there anything you need?"

"I am quite settled. I have everything I need and more. Everyone has been so welcoming."

"Good. I'm glad." He paused, then asked, "Has Brian been to see you?"

"No. But I didn't expect him to come to Gibeon any time soon. He has ranch work to do and his own family to care for."

"Still, you must miss them."

He was right, of course. She'd had six wonderful days with Brian, Kit, and the baby at Eden's Gate. But she'd known that was a temporary situation. She didn't expect to see him often, even though she lived only a couple of hours away. But at least she would see him several times a year, which was far more than she would have if she'd returned to Boston.

"I do miss them," she answered at last. "I know little Grayson will be growing up so fast. But I've met so many other people this week. Townsfolk. Parents of students. I won't be lonely." She thought of Hope, curled up in an orange and white ball on a blanket in a crate back in her little house, and she smiled. "I'm already making friends."

"Glad to hear it."

They entered the Hathaway house through a side door, walking into a parlor that was modest in size but seemed determined to hold the entire contents of a much grander house. Every surface bore evidence of Margaret's fondness for displaying her treasures. Victoria found it a little overwhelming. Still, she had the sense that this parlor had witnessed laughter, conversation, and the everyday moments that made up a life, and it gave her an entirely different perspective of the no-nonsense woman who ran the general store and post office with such efficiency.

Margaret made a sweeping motion with her hand. "Please make yourselves comfortable. I will ask Cook how long it will be before our dinner is ready."

Her husband, Harry, stood near the large fireplace, one elbow resting on the edge of the mantel, watching as their guests found places to sit. Victoria moved toward the black horsehair settee beneath the front window, its high back and scrolled arms stiff with dignity. She sat with care, mindful not to slide on the slick fabric, and leaned her back against a plump crocheted cushion.

"May I join you?" Reverend Blankenship asked.

"Of course."

He settled on the opposite end of the settee, then looked toward their host. "Stephen and Bertha weren't in church today," he said, referring to Harry and Margaret's son and daughter-in-law.

"No, Stephen had business in Pocatello, and Bertha accompanied him."

"Ah. I pray they have a safe trip."

Victoria was about to mention the delicious fruit pie Bertha had brought to her earlier in the week but was interrupted by Margaret's return.

"Our dinner is ready," she announced. "Please, all of you, come to the table."

The reverend stood and offered a hand to Victoria to help her rise. Then he motioned for her to precede him through the crowded parlor and into the adjoining dining room. Once there, he pulled out a chair for her before sitting on the one next to her. Harry and Margaret sat at the head and foot of the table, while Roger and William sat across from Victoria and Reverend Blankenship. Victoria tried not to be disappointed that Roger wasn't the one beside her.

ROGER WASN'T happy with the seating arrangement. He should have been the one escorting Victoria into the dining room. Then he could have been at her side throughout the meal.

A woman wearing a white cap and apron delivered covered dishes to the table set with china and crystal. Unexpected elegance, Roger thought. Before leaving the room, the cook removed the covers and took them to the sideboard.

Roger saw at once that this was no ordinary Sunday dinner. A roast duck glistened beneath a delicate glaze, accompanied by tender scalloped potatoes rich with cream and cheese. Glazed carrots, green peas with pearl onions, and a fragrant apple slaw filled the table with color and scent. Every dish, from the pickled onions on the cut-glass tray to the warm brioche rolls, spoke of Margaret's pride—not only in her table, but in the reach of her husband's mercantile.

Bowls and platters were passed around the table, and a gentle hum of conversation filled the room as the meal progressed. Roger tried to focus on the food on the plate before him, but his attention drifted across the table. And not for the first time.

Truman was speaking to Victoria. Again. Of course he was. Whatever he'd just said caused her to smile and tilt her head to one side. Then she laughed softly, her eyes bright.

Roger stabbed a pearl onion and brought it to his mouth with unnecessary force.

He liked Truman. Respected him, even. The man had a gentle manner and a well-read mind. He wasn't a showy preacher. Not the kind of man who called attention to himself. But still. There he was, sitting far too close to Victoria, almost whispering in her ear.

Margaret's voice carried down the table. "Reverend, you must tell us about the children's Bible lessons. Victoria, you'll appreciate this—he's been using chalk illustrations on a slate board. The little ones are completely captivated. Perhaps he can draw some for your class when school begins."

Victoria looked at Truman. "That's marvelous. I imagine it helps them remember the stories."

"Oh, it does. Although my attempts at drawing sheep have been called into question more than once." He turned from Victoria to glance across the table. "That wouldn't be an issue for you, Mr. Bernhardt. Perhaps you could give me a lesson or two."

Another round of laughter. Even William chuckled, shaking his head as he reached for his water glass.

Roger forced a smile. "I could try, I daresay." He hoped he didn't sound as irritated as he felt. And he knew exactly why he was annoyed, although he refused to put a name to it.

His thoughts were interrupted by firm footsteps and the creak of the swinging door. The cook entered the dining room again, this time carrying a tall confection on a wide porcelain platter.

The conversation quieted.

"Margaret," Harry said, admiration in his voice, "you've outdone yourself."

His wife beamed. "Cook deserves the credit, dear. She created exactly what I requested. Lemon jelly cake. Layers of sponge, lemon curd, and raspberry preserve. I do hope you all left room for it."

Roger glanced at Victoria as her eyes lit up in delight. She turned to Truman again, saying something Roger couldn't hear. He looked down at his plate, smiled faintly to himself, and silently named the blasted emotion.

He was jealous.

And he didn't like it one bit.

WHILE WILLIAM WENT to water the buggy horse before he and Roger began the trip back to Eden's Gate, Victoria was escorted home by Roger and Truman.

It seemed silly to her that both men insisted on accompanying her. She'd spent the last week walking alone all over this small town and even to a few outlying farms. She could certainly have made it from the general store on Main Street to the house tucked in the trees behind the school without getting lost or having a mishap.

"Are you studying for your exams?" Truman asked as they approached her new home. "My offer to help still stands. Whenever you need me."

"I haven't begun yet. My head has been too full of preparations for the start of school."

"Of course. Of course."

Roger asked, "What exams are those?"

She looked in his direction. "I thought you knew. My appointment as teacher for the Gibeon school is temporary. I will have to obtain my teaching certificate in order to continue beyond the next few months."

"Or possibly the entire school year," Truman interjected. "The lack of a teacher is considered an emergency situation."

Victoria nodded. "If I am ready, I will take the exams in October. If not, then I will have to test no later than in the spring."

"You'll be ready," Roger said, certainty in his voice.

She warmed at his words. His confidence in her mattered.

"Of course, she will," Truman agreed. "It's why we asked her to fill the position."

She saw a frown furrow Roger's forehead.

At the house, she stepped onto the porch, then turned to face her escorts. "Thank you both for seeing me home. You're most kind."

Neither man spoke. Neither man moved except to look at the other. For one ridiculous moment, she almost expected them to begin wrestling like a couple of boys in the schoolyard.

"I had best go in," she said. "Hope will be hungry."

"Hope?" They responded in unison.

"My kitten. I found her last night, half-starved to death. We've already become fast friends."

"You're keeping a stray cat in your house?" Truman gave his head a slight shake, the set of his mouth showing disapproval. "It could have fleas."

She stiffened, as if he'd insulted her and not the kitten. "Hope *doesn't* have fleas."

"I hope not, for your sake." He tugged on the wide brim of his black hat. "Do let me know if you need anything, Miss Castleton. I'm never too far away." He glanced at Roger. "Good day, Mr. Bernhardt."

"Good day, reverend." Roger turned immediately toward Victoria. "I would love to meet your kitten, if you don't think it would frighten her."

It was quite silly, she supposed, the way her pulse quickened at his simple request. Except for the short walk from the church to the Hathaway home, she'd scarcely had a moment to speak to him since leaving the ranch. The reverend had engaged her in conversation throughout the meal. Not that she'd minded talking with Truman. He was an interesting man. But Roger

. . .

"It won't," she answered. "Do come in." She led the way inside, happy that they would have at least a few moments together, just the two of them, before William arrived with the horse and buggy. But her pleasure soon vanished, replaced by a sense of loss. The kitten wasn't in the box. She leaned over and pushed the blanket this way and that. "She's not here."

"Don't worry. She's in the house somewhere, and there aren't that many places for her to hide."

As if in response to Roger's words, a strident *meow* drew their gazes toward the bedroom. Victoria hurried in that direction, pushing the door the rest of the way open to reveal Hope on top of the bureau, looking as if she wanted to get down but was afraid to jump from that height.

"*Meow.*"

"How on earth did you get up there?" She took the kitten into her arms and carried her back to the parlor.

Roger stroked the kitten with an index finger. "She'll be a beauty when she puts on a bit of weight."

"I think she's pretty now." She rubbed her cheek against Hope's head. "And she *doesn't* have fleas."

He chuckled. "I would never dare to suggest it."

She returned his smile—and for a second hoped he would lean in and kiss her.

His expression sobered. "You're going to be happy here."

"I believe so."

"You'll make Gibeon your home."

"That's my hope."

Something flickered behind his eyes. She sensed there was more he wanted to say or perhaps ask. Something important. But the sound of footsteps on the porch caused him to take a step back from her.

William rapped on the doorjamb. "Roger, you ready to head out?"

He looked at Victoria several heartbeats before answering, "I'm ready." A small smile returned. "I like your kitten, Victoria. You two take care of each other."

Chapter Twenty-Six

T he next morning, Roger took his sketchbook and pencils and rode north, hoping to force his thoughts somewhere other than to a particular hazel-eyed woman with a gold and white kitten in her arms. Before long, he saw the twisted tree that he'd sketched several times already. It was an intriguing subject, and he wasn't completely pleased with his earlier efforts. Perhaps today would be different.

Still on horseback, he circled the tree and the outcropping of rocks it grew beside until he found the right lighting.

After dismounting, he tethered the horse so it wouldn't wander too far while he worked. If he was fortunate, he would forget the horse and the world around him as he sketched. If he was fortunate, he would think of nothing but that crooked tree.

Sketchbook in hand, he settled onto the ground and began to draw. The first strokes of the pencil could have been of the tree, but in his mind's eye, he saw Victoria as she'd been the day she arrived in Gardiner. He remembered thinking she wasn't beautiful, that her face was too narrow, her nose too long, and her chin too sharp. What utter rubbish! She was more beautiful than any woman he'd ever known.

He thought back to the kiss they'd shared as they stood in the parlor of the guest cottage. More than a week had passed since then, and yet he could still feel the earth shake beneath his feet as it had when their lips met.

He groaned and his pencil stilled.

She would be happy living in Gibeon. He was sure of it. She would love being a teacher. She would mesh with the rhythm of life there.

Another memory pushed in. One from yesterday. The sight of Reverend Truman Blankenship muttering something softly near Victoria's ear. Of her corresponding smile and the music of her laughter.

He growled this time, put sketchbook and pencil on the ground, and rose to his feet. He strode to the tree, put his hand on the bark, looked up at its branches, wanting to get an artist's view. Enough to inspire him.

What a pretense! He didn't want to look at the tree. He didn't want to sketch it either. He wanted to look at Victoria, to be with her, to hear her voice and listen to her laughter. But he had no right to disturb the life she wanted to make for herself.

"Don't you suppose you should talk to her about it?"

Okay, perhaps William was right about that. Perhaps Roger should let Victoria know the depth of his feelings. He'd admitted to himself that he loved her, but she might not know how he felt. Still, loving her didn't change the facts. If he wanted them to have a life together, it wouldn't be a life spent in one place. There was so much more of this great country to see, so many more wonderful things in nature for him to paint.

"Your father sounds like a sensible man."

Victoria had spoken those words to him the first day they'd met, and he'd understood the feelings behind the sentiment. He understood them even more now. If he loved her—and he did—he should let her find happiness with a man more suited to her. A man like Truman Blankenship, who had obviously taken a real interest in her now that she was living in town.

"Do let me know if you need anything, Miss Castleton. I'm never too far away."

Blast the reverend! The church and parsonage were entirely too close to the teacher's house.

Roger ground his teeth as he turned and strode back to his sketchbook. He would draw that tree and he would get it right, and he wouldn't think about Victoria for the remainder of the morning. So help him, he wouldn't.

VICTORIA WAS WRITING on the blackboard when a loud clap of thunder shook the schoolhouse. She squealed as she spun around. The chalk in her hand clattered to the floor and broke into several pieces. Only then did she realize how dark the interior of the building had become while she was concentrating on the lesson she planned to share the first day of school.

She picked up the broken chalk, then moved down the aisle between desks, passed through the cloakroom, and stood in the open doorway, watching as the wind bent trees toward the east. Leaves twirled and spun through the air. She saw men and women, hands atop their hats and bonnets, hurrying down the boardwalk or disappearing inside businesses.

"I had better get home before—" A flash of light and another crash of thunder interrupted her words. And on its heels came the rain.

Blessed, blessed rain.

She imagined William standing in the barnyard with his face turned toward the heavens, thanking God for the sudden downpour. She closed her eyes and thanked Him too. Was it too much to hope that it would rain for hours? Or perhaps the storms could come in waves over several days. That would be even better.

Of course, days of rain would make things miserable for the cowboys who worked on the ranches. Or for anyone who might want to come into town for some reason. Someone like Mrs. Adler or . . . or Roger.

A gust of wind pushed rain toward the doorway, misting her face and clothes. It reminded her of the storm in Yellowstone that had swept in as she and Roger walked by the lake. She recalled the wind tugging at her skirts and pulling at her hat. Mostly she remembered the way Roger had taken her arm and hurried her toward the porch of the hotel, just in time to keep them from getting soaked.

In the distance, a fork of lightning darted from black clouds to earth. The resounding thunder arrived seconds later, once again shaking the schoolhouse, once again causing her to jump in alarm. She leaned forward and looked toward the west. If the sky was any indication, this rain wouldn't let up for a long while yet.

<hr>

ROGER RODE INTO THE BARNYARD, looking for all the world—he was certain—like a drowned rat. He just hoped the leather saddlebag had managed to keep his sketchbook dry because he'd been pleased with his final drawing of the old misshapen tree. He'd finished that last sketch only moments before the first flash of lightning split the dark heavens.

Once inside the barn, he dismounted and gave the horse a few firm pats on the neck. "We made it, old chap."

After hanging the saddlebags on a post, he unsaddled the gray gelding, gave him a good rub down, and put him into a stall with a scoop of grain along with a bucket of water. As he closed the stall gate, he heard hoofbeats striking the ground and a man's *whoop* a few moments before William and two of his men rode into the barn.

If they were any indication, Roger *definitely* resembled a drowned rat.

William swept off his hat, sending rainwater spraying in Roger's direction. "Glory hallelujah!" he shouted. "Let it rain!" He dropped to the ground.

His friend's exuberance made him grin.

"Looks like you got caught in it too." William led his horse toward an empty stall. "Did you go to town?"

"No. I was doing some sketching near the north boundary."

William flipped up the stirrup and began to loosen the cinch. "Thought you might have gone to town."

"I have no reason to go to town."

"Haven't you?" William glanced over his shoulder.

"No." Roger took the saddlebags from the post. "I haven't."

William shook his head, then pulled the saddle and blanket from the horse's back. "If you say so." He laughed.

Roger set his jaw. Why say more? They both knew he was avoiding the truth. He had a very good reason to want to go to town. But he had decided there was an even better reason to avoid doing so.

"You know, Roger." William's smile was gone now, no sign of the laughter remaining in his gaze. "You will have to make up your mind, one way or the other."

He'd made up his mind. At least, he thought he had. Despite loving Victoria, the best thing for both of them was for him to leave her be. The best thing would be for him to stick with his own plans. The ones he'd made right after the death of his father and the sale of the drapery business. He was footloose. He needed to remain so.

Chapter Twenty-Seven

Several days later, Roger stood at the edge of the barnyard, brush in hand, staring at the morning light as it filtered through the trees. He'd been there long enough for the shadows to shift and for the sun to climb higher in the pale late-summer sky. The crunch of boots on dry grass alerted him to the presence of another. William never moved like a man who had anything to hide.

"You've painted that stand of trees before," his friend said. "Do they speak to you or are you just avoiding someone who can *really* speak to you?"

He didn't answer, only dabbed his brush into a murky brown and dabbed at a canvas that didn't deserve the effort. The colors weren't right. The light felt wrong. Or maybe it was him that felt wrong.

William waited a long moment. Then, with characteristic directness, he said, "You ever plan on telling her how you feel?"

Roger let the brush still in his hand. "You already asked me that."

"No. What I asked you before was whether you supposed you ought to talk to her about it. This time I'm asking whether you ever plan to."

The difference hung heavy between them.

"It wouldn't change anything. She's making a life in Gibeon. She has her family nearby, and she'll have her teaching. She belongs where she is."

William crossed his arms, jaw tightening. "You shouldn't get to decide that for her."

"I'm not—"

"Yes, you are. You're walking away and calling it sacrifice. That's tidy, I suppose. Noble even. But it isn't honest."

Roger bristled. "She wants roots. Order. Children one day, I'd imagine. I can't offer her those things."

"You haven't offered her anything. You kissed her, didn't you? The day before she moved to town?"

Roger didn't ask how William knew.

"And she kissed you back."

He gave a terse nod.

"Then what exactly are you doing here?" William waved an arm. "Painting trees you've painted already, wandering Eden's Gate like a ghost while the woman you love is less than an hour away and thinks you've forgotten her."

Roger's throat tightened. "She doesn't think that. I was with her on Sunday."

"She'll think it soon enough."

The silence between them settled like dust.

Roger turned his eyes back to the trees, but they held no magic for him. "I got a letter yesterday. Jake brought it from town. It's an offer of a new commission. There's a hotel that wants me to paint a large landscape for its lobby. It pays rather well. I'd have to leave in a few days, and I'd be gone for a couple of weeks. Perhaps three. I haven't said yes yet, but I believe I will."

"You need to talk to Victoria before you go."

He didn't answer.

William sighed and looked at the sky. "Roger, we haven't known each other for long. Just over a year. But that's long enough for me to know you like freedom and open spaces. You don't want to be tied down in traditional ways. I might even say you're a lot like Isaiah Coltrane."

He laughed. "Me? Like Isaiah? You are wrong about that, I daresay. He may prefer to live in the wilderness and track poachers in the national park. But that man has deep roots, ones that will only deepen once he and Amanda have children."

"Children?" William cocked an eyebrow. "Do you know something I don't?"

"No. It was merely an observation."

William grunted. "Whether or not you are like Isaiah doesn't matter. Just don't walk away from Victoria while telling yourself it's for her sake. She deserves more than that from you. She deserves the truth."

"And if the truth doesn't solve anything?"

"Then at least you'll know you tried. And she'll

know what she meant to you. That's better than silence."

Is it? The question echoed in Roger's mind as William walked away, leaving him alone with his thoughts and a canvas he could no longer see clearly.

———

VICTORIA SLICED a peach into a shallow bowl, watching the golden slivers tumble over a piece of cold cornbread. She'd already boiled an egg and filled a glass with water from the pump. Simple fare, but enough. Her head ached faintly from hours spent squinting over lesson plans and the daunting manual on Idaho teaching standards.

She stepped onto the porch, grateful for the breath of air stirring the grass. The heat was climbing again, bold and relentless, as if the brief respite of rain three days before had never happened. The road into town was already dry and chalky.

Hope leapt up beside her on the porch rail, tail flicking.

Victoria smiled, scratching under the kitten's chin. "I believe you're the only soul who hasn't asked how my studies are going." She settled into the creaking chair with her plate on her lap. "Or if I'm nervous about the start of school."

The kitten yawned, showing her tiny pink tongue.

Victoria let her gaze drift to the schoolyard, barely visible through the trees. Four more days. The enormity of it made her chest tighten. She had never stood before a group of children to instruct them in anything. What if they saw through her inexperience? What if she failed?

A breeze passed over the porch, and she closed her eyes briefly, letting it cool her temples.

The sound of footsteps on the path made her sit up straighter. Hope scrambled off the rail and darted beneath the chair. A moment later, Reverend Blankenship appeared through the trees, smiling beneath the brim of his straw hat.

"Miss Castleton," he called, raising a hand.

She set her plate aside, brushing crumbs from her skirt. "Reverend. What a pleasant surprise."

"I hope I'm not intruding. I went to the school but you weren't there. You mentioned needing help with the section on American history."

"Of course." She motioned to the other chair. "Would you like to sit a moment?"

"Thank you." He stepped onto the porch, glancing down as Hope darted past him. "You decided to keep the cat?" Surprise tinged the question.

"Yes."

He frowned as the kitten disappeared into the house. "Cats are independent creatures. Not always suited to domestic life. She would be better off in a barn, chasing mice."

"I disagree. She is better off with me." Victoria reached for her plate again, pulling a last piece of peach free with her fingers and placing it carefully on the porch railing for the kitten when she returned. "Hope didn't object to the bath I gave her, in case she had fleas." She chuckled softly. "Although I can't say she enjoyed it either."

Truman made a sound in his throat, then removed a sheaf of folded papers from his coat pocket. "I brought a few notes that might help you study for the American history exam. Key dates, particularly for the constitutional period. You'll want to memorize those."

She took the pages with a murmur of thanks. After putting on her spectacles, she scanned the handwriting. He wrote in firm, straight lines—methodical, like the man himself.

"I appreciate your help, Reverend Blankenship. Studying for my teaching certificate . . . Well, it's so long since I was in school myself. It's quite intimidating to think about it."

"You'll be ready. You're disciplined, and you don't shrink from hard work. That will carry you through."

She looked up, removed her glasses, and smiled at him. "That's kind of you to say."

He cleared his throat and shifted in his seat. "Victoria . . ." He had never used her given name before, and the sound of it now made her still. He didn't look at her. He stared out at the schoolyard beyond the trees, where a bird darted low across the grass. "I admire your courage. Leaving everything familiar behind. Beginning again."

She waited.

"I know you've got a great deal on your mind with the school year beginning. And I don't wish to press you. But I want you to know that if you ever need more than a study partner or a friend—"

"Reverend—"

He held up a hand. "Let me finish, please."

She nodded.

"I think very highly of you. And I believe, in time, we could build something steady and good together. You needn't answer now. I only ask that you consider it." His gaze met hers at last.

Victoria felt a weight settle in her chest—not of pressure, but of regret. "I am honored by your words, sir. And I'm grateful for your friendship. Truly. But I would not wish to give you hope where there is none."

"Is there . . . someone else?"

Was there someone else? She saw Roger in her mind. Heard his voice as he described the world around them. Felt his lips touch hers as a hand drew her closer. He was a man filled with dreams, a man who didn't want to settle down or stay in one place, a man who didn't mind uncertainty. How reckless it would be to love someone like him. "No," she whispered at last. "But neither is my heart free to give to you."

Another silence stretched between them.

Finally, Truman stood. "I appreciate your honesty, Miss Castleton."

"And I appreciate your kindness." She set aside the plate and rose as well.

He offered a small smile. "If ever you change your mind—"

"I will always value your friendship, Reverend Blankenship."

He gave a slight bow of his head and turned to go.

As his footsteps faded, Hope slipped silently out from

the house and pressed her side against Victoria's skirts. Leaning down, Victoria picked up the kitten, then rubbed her cheek against the feline's soft fur, her throat tight.

She had spoken truthfully. Her heart was not free to give. It belonged to another already. And it would go with him when he went away.

Chapter Twenty-Eight

When Victoria stepped out of her little house the following morning, a basket hanging from the crook of her arm, she was met with a refreshing breeze that seemed to promise cooler mornings for the remainder of summer. Or perhaps that was wishful thinking.

As she crossed Main Street on her way to the general store, she saw a horse tied outside the telegraph office. The tall gray seemed familiar. It looked like one of the Overstreet horses. Perhaps William was inside, sending a telegram. Or an Eden's Gate ranch hand.

That's when Roger stepped out of the office onto the boardwalk, settling his hat onto his head with one hand while closing the door behind him. Victoria's pulse quickened. It had only been five days since they'd sat across from each other in the Hathaway dining room, but it felt far longer to her. When he looked toward her, he seemed to hesitate, as if unsure what to do next. Then he strode in her direction. She stepped onto the boardwalk outside the mercantile and waited for him to reach her, heart hammering.

"Good morning." His smile didn't quite reach his eyes.

In her memory, she heard Truman ask, *"Is there . . . someone else?"*

She wanted there to be, foolish though it was. "Good morning." Her reply was almost too soft to hear.

"How have you been? Are you ready for the start of school?"

"As ready as I can be."

"And your kitten?"

She smiled, glad he had thought to ask about Hope. "She is already putting on weight. Not nearly so skinny as she was."

"Good. Glad to hear it." His own smile seemed more genuine now.

Several heartbeats passed.

Victoria drew a quick breath. "Were you sending a telegram?"

"I was, as it happens. I've been offered a commission by a hotel in Pocatello."

You're leaving? her mind shouted. But with her mouth, she said, "That's wonderful. Your art is becoming known. That hotel is wise to hire you now while they can still afford to feature your work." And again her mind shouted, *Will you return?*

Roger released an abrupt laugh. "I suppose that is the dream of artists everywhere. For their art to be in great demand."

"You have so many paintings still at the ranch. I saw

them in the shed and in the cottage. Just stored away where no one can see them. What will you do with those? It isn't just the Kennedys or visitors to that gallery in Rhode Island who should enjoy them." She sounded foolish, even in her own ears, but she couldn't seem to help herself. "You could have a showing here in Gibeon. I would be glad to help you arrange it. Perhaps it could be held at the school on a Saturday."

Anything to keep you here.

Oh, the foolishness of it.

She lowered her gaze to the boardwalk, embarrassed by her rush of words, embarrassed by wanting so desperately to find a way to keep Roger in Gibeon. But the world awaited him. Surely fame awaited him. What had she to offer that could change his mind about chasing that dream?

He didn't answer right away, and she lifted her eyes enough to see that he was studying her, his expression unreadable.

"I don't think a showing here would suit," he said at last.

"Oh." Her voice was small. "Of course. I didn't mean to presume."

His jaw tightened, almost imperceptibly. "You weren't presuming."

She wrapped her fingers more tightly around the handle of the basket. Inside were her coin purse, a folded list, and a small bundle of dried lavender for Margaret Hathaway. She focused on those items instead of the emptiness creeping into her chest.

He said, "I only meant that I don't think I'll be here long enough to make it worth the effort."

There it was. Confirmation. He was leaving.

"You're going to Pocatello," she said, keeping her voice even. "And after that?"

He shrugged, the movement casual. "I'll see where the road leads."

And she—who had never liked the notion of roads without destinations—nodded as if she understood. But she didn't. Not really. "Brian used to be like that too."

He gave his head a slight shake. "What do you mean?"

"I mean . . . he wanted to pack his sketchbooks and leave. Nothing planned. No map of where he wanted to go or plans for how long he meant to stay in one place. He didn't want to build anything permanent."

"Well, he's building something permanent now. He and Kit with the baby."

She swallowed a lump forming in her throat. "Yes, he found something better than the road."

"Better than the road," he echoed softly.

They stood in silence as someone exited the general store behind her, murmuring a polite greeting as they passed. A wagon rattled by on the street. Somewhere in the distance, a door slammed.

"We kissed," she whispered. "Did it mean anything to you?"

"It meant something."

"But not enough to stay in Gibeon. Not enough to tell me what you feel."

"I didn't know what to say." He drew a breath and let it out slowly. "My feelings won't change anything."

"How do you know? Must you make that decision alone?" Her words hung in the air, too direct, too sharp. She regretted them and didn't, all at once.

He took a half-step back. "You're making a life here, Victoria. You have your family close, a new place in this community. If I stayed a little longer, I wouldn't be doing you any favors."

"Are you trying to protect me from my own feelings?"

"I'm trying to be fair. To do right by you."

Tears welled in her eyes, but she refused to let them fall. "No, you're being selfish and pretending it's concern for me."

He flinched. It was slight, but she saw it.

"I thought . . ." Her voice thinned. "I thought you cared about me."

"I do."

"Then why won't you stay?"

For a moment, he said nothing. Then, at last, "I'm not meant to stay, Victoria. I don't want a life that is planned out for me. My father planned out my life, almost from the day I was born. I do not want anyone else doing that."

She nodded slowly, as if she hadn't just felt her heart shatter in her chest, as if his words hadn't cut her like a sharp knife through a loaf of soft bread.

"Victoria, I wish—"

"Please don't say you wish things were different."

She lifted her chin and blinked away the tears. "You want to go. You should go."

He studied her for another moment. Then he inclined his head slightly. "I hope it goes well for you. I really do." He stepped off the boardwalk and walked back in the direction of the telegraph office and the gray gelding he'd ridden into town.

She watched him leave, her heart aching with a pain she hadn't expected to feel so keenly. She stood very still until he mounted the horse and rode out of town. Only then did she turn into the mercantile, blinking hard against another wave of tears, the basket clenched tightly in her hand.

She had three days to be ready for the school-children.

And somehow, she had to be ready for a life without Roger Bernhardt, too.

Chapter Twenty-Nine

The hired coach left Eden's Gate before dawn the following morning. Roger sat stiff-backed on the worn seat, one hand braced against the window frame to steady himself as the coach rocked and swayed over the hard earth. His satchel lay at his feet, half-full of sketchbooks and pencils. The remainder of his supplies —paints, canvas rolls, folding easel—were lashed to the top of the coach, likely being knocked about with every jolt. He hadn't had the presence of mind to supervise their stowage with his usual care.

His gaze drifted to the window, though he saw little beyond it. Darkness still blanketed the world. It mattered little. His thoughts were still in Gibeon.

Still on the boardwalk.

Still looking into Victoria's eyes as she asked him the one thing he could not answer. *Then why won't you stay?*

He'd offered nothing but excuses. He wasn't meant to stay. He wouldn't do her any favors by lingering. He wanted to be fair, to do right by her. He thought it better to leave now, before she built her life around a man who didn't know how to stand still.

"Please don't say you wish things were different. You want to go. You should go."

She was right. He'd made his choice. But he wasn't trying to do right by her or to protect her. He'd chosen to go because he was a coward.

He exhaled slowly and shifted his shoulders against the padded seat.

"You want to go. You should go."

Her words had followed him from the mercantile, to the telegraph office, and all the way back to Eden's Gate. They echoed still, like a bell he couldn't stop ringing. He rubbed his forehead with his thumb. How had it come to this?

He'd spent most of his life fulfilling someone else's plan. From the moment he could hold a tape measure, his father had instructed him in the art of assessing fabric, calculating yardage, memorizing stock ledgers. Peter Bernhardt had taken great pride in his work and greater pride in the business he'd built. Bernhardt & Son. Roger had been the son, of course. The heir. The one meant to inherit and make the business even better. Whether he wished it or not.

As a boy, his sketches had been dismissed with a wave. His paintings were considered "a bit of play." His commendation in the Royal Drawing Society's youth exhibition had been met with a pat on the shoulder and an admonition not to let it "go to his head." His father hadn't been a cruel man, only a rigid one. Practical to the core, with no tolerance for dreams not tied directly to commerce or advantage. He had suggested—no, declared—that Roger should settle down, that he might look to marry the daughter of a haberdasher with whom the Bernhardts had longstanding ties. A respectable girl. Pretty enough. Dowry in hand. None of this artistic nonsense.

Selling the drapery business after the accident that killed his father had been an easy thing to do. He loved America and he'd wanted freedom. Now he had both.

But did he want freedom any longer? And was it truly freedom if he kept running from anything with weight? Anything that might tie him to one place?

Victoria had offered him nothing more than herself. Not control. Not expectation. Just a seat at her side, if he wanted it. And he'd turned away.

"Are you trying to protect me from my own feelings?" Her voice, calm and wounded, rang in his mind.

Had he truly believed he was protecting her? Or had it always been about protecting himself?

He closed his eyes and leaned back, the coach rocking steadily beneath him. A dry wind slipped through the window, seeming to scrape his skin. He felt brittle. Everything felt brittle.

Roger imagined Victoria in the schoolhouse, bent over a lesson book, her spectacles perched on her nose. He imagined her kitten winding between her ankles as she made tea in the quiet of her little kitchen.

He'd thought himself unsuited to a life like that. But what if that life would suit him more than he realized?

A wheel dropped into a rut, slamming Roger's shoulder into the side of the coach, and his gaze flicked out at the passing hills, still gray in the dim light.

What if he turned back? What if he told her the truth—that he was afraid? Afraid he would fail her. Afraid of building something only to lose it. Afraid that he didn't know how to be the man she deserved.

But what if she already knew all that… and had chosen him anyway? What if she was willing to share him with his dreams? Could he make a home with Victoria in Gibeon, yet venture out on occasion, traveling to paint before returning to her? Wasn't that better than nothing at all?

"You want to go. You should go."

He reached into the satchel at his feet and pulled out his sketchbook. Inside, between pages of distant ridges and cottonwoods in shifting light, was a pencil study of Victoria. It wasn't finished. He hadn't needed it to be. The tilt of her chin, the focus in her eyes, the way her hair curled near the nape of her neck. He'd drawn it from memory one quiet evening after she'd moved into Gibeon. His throat tightened as he closed the book and rested it on his lap.

And for the first time since his father's death, Roger Bernhardt wondered if freedom had less to do with choosing the open road and more to do with choosing someone on purpose. Someone like Victoria.

Victoria awakened on Saturday morning with a heaviness in her chest that no amount of stretching or tea could dispel. Light filtered through the curtains, dim and grayish, not the usual golden wash of late August mornings. For a moment, she lay still beneath the thin sheet, listening to the sound of a breeze moving the branches outside. But the air carried no comfort this morning. It whispered of change, of something unsettled.

She sat up, smoothing her hand over the coverlet. She hadn't slept well. Her dreams had been scattered, shadows of yesterday's conversation with Roger threading through her mind. *"You want to go. You should go."* She'd said it like a woman certain she would be okay after he left. But she wasn't certain at all.

She rose, wrapped herself in a light robe, and crossed through the parlor to open the front door. Hope padded out from beneath the settee and rubbed against her ankles, and she bent down to lift the kitten to her chest.

"We'll be all right," she crooned softly, rubbing her cheek against Hope's fur.

She stepped onto the porch, the wood cool beneath her bare feet. Through the tree branches, she could see clouds, high and dark, as though layered upon themselves in streaks. They looked ominous in a way she couldn't describe. She'd lived through several storms since arriving in the west, but this sky looked different, strange. Even the light seemed wrong. A gust of wind, dry and abrasive, tugged at her loose hair.

She shivered, though the air was warm.

Hope struggled against her. When Victoria set her down, the kitten bounded down the steps and pounced at a beetle skittering across the dry-packed earth. Victoria watched her, half-smiling, but the unease didn't lift.

Perhaps her anxiety had more to do with her troubled dreams than with the stormy skies. Or perhaps it was because she felt as if Roger had taken a piece of her heart with him when he'd ridden out of town yesterday. A piece she would never be able to recover.

Silly, she supposed. She had suffered other losses and survived. She'd lost her childhood home and then her parents. Her brother had abandoned her. And yet she'd survived. Perhaps she'd even thrived.

But Roger . . . She felt lost without him even though she'd only known him for a couple of months.

Drawing in a long breath, she turned back into the house. After going to her bedroom to dress and ready herself for the day, she brewed a pot of tea. When she walked to the schoolhouse a short while later, the wind had picked up. It hissed at her through the eaves and caused loose leaves to flutter across her path. She unlocked the door, opening it wide. She wanted the children to arrive on Monday to a space that smelled of clean boards and chalk, not close summer heat and dust.

As she went to the teacher's desk at the front of the room, she heard the distant roll of thunder. Good. They would have more rain soon. William and the other ranchers and farmers in the area would be thankful for that.

What about Roger? Was he looking up at the sky, wishing he could paint those threatening clouds? Could he capture that odd color, where the air seemed to have turned yellow?

No. No, she wouldn't allow her thoughts to go there, to stay there.

She sat at the desk and pulled out the lesson plans she'd written over the course of the past week. After donning her spectacles, she went through them again, scarcely aware of the passage of time or the gusts of wind striking the side of the schoolhouse or the distant roll of thunder.

It was the loud clatter of hooves and wagon wheels that finally broke her concentration. Perhaps because it sounded urgent, so in contrast to a slow Saturday morning. She rose and went to the stoop in time to see a lathered horse slide to a halt in front of the mercantile. The driver of the battered farm wagon waved his hat in the air.

"Fire! There's a range fire west of town! Comin' this way!"

Victoria's stomach turned over and her gaze shot down Main Street.

"Lightning hit out near the Johnson place," the driver called as people hurried in his direction. "Dry strike. Lit the grass like kindling. Wind caught it, and it's movin' fast. Headed east and south both."

"The Johnson farm's only five miles from here," Harry Hathaway shouted.

"The fire's less than that now. Nothing to stop it neither. Just more fuel in its path."

As if to prove a point, the wind gusted again, harder this time, sending dirt spinning in dust devils down the street. Beyond it—far beyond it—a billow of smoke became obvious.

Harry burst away from the other men, running toward Victoria. What on earth? With barely a glance at her, he reached for the rope to the school bell and gave it a hard pull. Again and again and again. The ringing of the bell felt as if it clanged inside her chest.

"We'll need volunteers," someone across the street shouted above the noise of wind and bell. "Water lines, buckets, shovels. Get folks moving. We need to try to clear a break on the west end of town."

Victoria turned toward Harry. "How bad is it, truly? Will it reach the town?"

"If the wind holds like it is, the fire could pass north of us. But if it turns just a little bit to the south—" His words broke off, but he didn't need to finish.

Victoria's thoughts flew from the schoolhouse to the church to her little house with a kitten playing with a beetle near the porch. The thought of fire consuming it all stole the breath from her chest. "What can I do to help?" she managed to ask.

"We need every barrel and tub in town filled with water. Find Margaret. She'll tell you what to do. We've gotta soak linens and move whatever we can from the back of the buildings. Women and children will have to do that. The men are needed to clear a firebreak."

Without another word, she rushed down the schoolhouse steps and across the street. The others who had come running at the first cry of "fire" were dispersing, spreading the message to those now responding to the ringing bell.

"Tell me what to do," Victoria cried above the racket.

Margaret's brow was tight, her expression composed but pale. "We'll start with the general store. We've got barrels out back we can fill with water. And there's buckets in the store room. We'll want all of them."

Overhead, dark clouds swirled and built but refused to drop any rain. Another gust of wind rattled the shutters behind them. It brought with it the acrid scent of smoke. Faint but definitely there.

Oh, God. Help us!

Chapter Thirty

The wheels creaked as the coach rolled into the Eden's Gate's barnyard, the horses slick with sweat and dust after a long, hard turnabout. Roger leaned out the window as they came to a stop, his hand gripping the edge of the doorframe. The sky overhead was a strange, brassy color—light bleeding through heavy clouds in odd slants.

He didn't wait for the coach to come to a complete stop before he pushed open the door and hopped to the ground. He was about to stride toward the house when he caught sight of William near the corral fence, his hat shoved back on his head, eyes trained westward.

"Didn't expect to see you for a few weeks," he said as Roger approached.

"I had them turn around. Didn't even make it halfway to Pocatello before I knew I'd made a mistake."

William met his gaze. "I figured as much."

"Did you?"

"I did." A smile tugged at the corners of his mouth

but disappeared the moment his gaze returned to the west.

Roger looked toward the same distant ridge line. The wind was gusting harder now, dry as a bone. Not a drop of moisture in it. Light flashed in the distance.

"Lightning without rain," William muttered. "Sets a man's teeth on edge. Haven't liked the feel of things all morning."

"Cattle?"

"They'll spook if the sky so much as grumbles wrong. But it's not just them I'm worried about." His voice dropped. "This kind of weather? A fire could roll across this valley faster than a man can think."

As if to underscore the point, a hawk screeched overhead.

Chest tight, Roger said, "I need a horse."

"The gray's in a stall. Take him."

Roger was already moving, unbuttoning his coat as he went. Inside the barn, the shadows were cooler, but the air held the same tension. He moved on instinct—bridle, saddle, check the cinch. The gelding tossed his head, sensing the unrest.

By the time Roger rode out of the barn, William had climbed the fence and was scanning the sky again. The rumble of thunder reached their ears.

Roger didn't wait for more. He gave William a short nod, then turned the gray toward Gibeon and dug in his heels.

The horse surged forward. Dust swirled in the wind and scraped against Roger's face, but he barely noticed. His thoughts were ahead of him, reaching toward the little house tucked near the schoolhouse, the porch where a kitten liked to sun herself, the woman whose heart he'd bruised because he was too afraid to admit the truth.

He needed to reach her.

The road curved and opened onto a low ridge, and that's when he saw it.

Smoke. Thick and rising in billows, curling skyward with a hungry edge. In the distance. Definitely west of Gibeon, but with the wind in his face, it had to be driving the fire toward town.

He leaned low over the saddle and pressed the gelding harder.

Finally—it felt like an eternity—the town came into view. Minutes later, he saw people moving with purpose. Women and children. Buckets and barrels. Horses being hitched to wagons.

He recognized Margaret Hathaway first and rode toward her. "Where's Victoria?" he asked as he dropped from the saddle.

"I don't know. Helping somewhere." She met his gaze with an urgent one of her own. "Your hands'll be needed at the firebreak. Head to the other end of town."

He wanted to refuse. He wanted to search for Victoria.

Margaret added, "Harry said we might have a couple hours if the wind doesn't turn or whip up. Couple hours isn't much."

Roger didn't ask more. He set off running toward the west end of town.

Lord, keep her safe wherever she is. And let me get the chance to tell her how I feel.

As THE MORNING PROGRESSED, the smoke thickened, falling over Gibeon in layers. It stung Victoria's eyes and scraped the back of her throat with every breath. The wind gusted from the west, pushing the smoke into every corner. She couldn't see the schoolhouse at the other end of town. To be honest, she could barely see the feed store across the street.

She passed another dripping blanket to Caroline Drummond who hauled it up a ladder to drape over a west-facing awning on the doctor's porch. Somewhere behind her, someone coughed. She heard women calling out instructions to children. From somewhere deep within the smoke, men's voices shouted orders.

Victoria wiped soot from her cheeks with her sleeve. Her arms ached from carrying water buckets and soaked fabric. Her dress clung to her with sweat and smoke and grime. Still, she kept working. She didn't dare stop. The fire couldn't be far away now. Was the firebreak wide enough to save the town? To save the people and animals in it?

The animals. She thought of Hope. Was she safe? Had the bell ringing and the shouts of people frightened her? Had she run away? If so, would she run in the wrong direction.

A sudden, urgent need to check on her kitten

washed over her. She looked up at Caroline. "I'll be right back."

She ran down the dry-packed street. The wind whipped her skirts around her legs, causing her to stumble and nearly fall. Hastily, she grabbed the fabric with both hands and lifted it enough to stop it from tripping her. Her throat burned by the time she reached the porch of her home.

"Hope?" she called.

When Victoria had departed the house that morning, she'd left the door ajar because Hope was playing outside. It had blown open wide now.

"Kitty, kitty."

A small meow answered from beneath the porch.

Relief flooded through her as she dropped to her knees. "Kitty." Dim light filtered through the trees, and she caught the reflection of the kitten's eyes. "There you are, my sweet girl. Come out to me. You're safe now. I'm here."

Hope inched forward and soon she was nestled against Victoria's chest.

"Precious, kitty. It will be all right."

Something cracked overhead. She lifted her eyes in time to see a piece of trim tear loose from the house. An instant later, a sharp, stunning pain exploded on her forehead. The world swayed as she pitched forward, Hope leaping from her grip. The pain worsened, and then everything went black.

Victoria groaned. Her head thrummed with pain. Without opening her eyes—which she feared would worsen the pain—she lifted a hand to touch her forehead. But that was when she realized someone held her. Someone was carrying her.

"Miss Castleton?"

She knew that voice. It was . . . it was . . . Truman Blankenship. She opened her eyes, and Truman's blurry face appeared above her. He gave her a tight smile.

"What . . . what happened?" she whispered.

"You were hit in the head. I think it was a board off the corner of your house."

He set her down. Only then did she realize he had carried her onto her front porch and put her on the chair.

She frowned. "What is that sound?"

His smile was in earnest now as he knelt beside her chair. "Rain."

"Rain?" She blinked and turned her head away from him, ignoring the throbbing. The falling rain was as heavy as the smoke had been not that long ago.

"Yes, rain."

"And the fire?"

"It's stopped at the firebreak. Looks like the rain is extinguishing it."

She closed her eyes again, listening to the raindrops hitting the leaves of the trees and the roof of the porch. It was the most beautiful sound she'd ever heard.

"How are you feeling?" Truman asked, intruding on her private joy.

She touched her forehead with her fingertips. "My head hurts, but I think I'm all right."

"It was only by God's grace I saw you on the ground as I was leaving the church."

"Yes." She looked at him. "And I am grateful. I came to look for Hope and—" At that exact moment, the kitten leaped into Victoria's lap. Hope's unexpected appearance made Victoria laugh, despite the jolt of pain it caused. "There you are."

As she lifted the kitten close to her chin, her gaze caught movement coming through the trees.

Perhaps she wasn't all right. She was seeing things. It looked like Roger striding toward her on the narrow pathway. But it couldn't be him.

And yet, it was.

He was soaked to the skin, his shirt clinging to him, his hands blackened with soot. His pale hair was plastered to his head, and his eyes—those deep, searching blue eyes—were locked on her. He stopped short a few paces away, taking in the sight of Truman kneeling at her side.

Victoria's heart skipped a beat as she saw the way his expression changed. The way he drew back ever so slightly. She remembered him turning away on the boardwalk yesterday. Had it been only yesterday? It seemed so much longer ago than that.

But he didn't turn away again. He didn't leave. Instead, he stepped forward, dropping to a crouch beside the two of them, his eyes never leaving hers. "I came as soon as I could," he said quietly, his voice raw.

"I wanted to find you, but they needed men for the firebreak."

Her breath caught. "I thought you'd gone."

"I had. But I came back."

A long pause passed between them.

Truman stood slowly, perhaps reading the moment for what it was. "I'll check on the others, now that there's someone here to look after you."

Victoria didn't take her eyes off Roger. "You came back."

"I couldn't go forward without you. Turns out, I don't want a hundred new landscapes. I want one place. The place next to you. Wherever that may be."

Her throat ached for a different reason now.

"If you'll have me," he added.

"Yes." The word came out like a breath and a prayer and a promise all in one.

"I love you, Victoria Castleton."

"And I love you, Roger Bernhardt."

The wind quieted, but the rain kept falling, washing away the fire and smoke—and any doubts of what the future might bring.

Epilogue

Eden's Gate Ranch
March 1897

The sun hung low in the western sky, casting a golden glow across the pastures and painting remaining patches of snow in tones of rose and amber. The cold still lingered in the shadows, but there was no mistaking it now. Spring was on its way.

Roger stood at the fence, gloved hands resting on the top rail, watching two colts chase each other across the muddy paddock. Their long legs moved awkwardly, still learning what to do with all that energy. A calf bawled somewhere farther off, its mother answering with a low, contented sound.

The world smelled of thawing earth, dried alfalfa hay, and promise.

Behind him, the ranch house was warm and full of laughter. Supper had ended nearly an hour ago, but everyone except Roger still sat around the table. When he'd excused himself, Kit was cradling baby Grayson on her lap while Isaiah was about to recount another tale about his second winter in Montana with Amanda. Amanda sat beside her husband, looking nothing like the English noblewoman who first arrived at Eden's Gate and more like a woman who had well and truly found her footing. As for Victoria—Roger's bride of over four months now—she had been laughing over something William said.

Even a year ago, Roger hadn't known what it would be like to be part of something like this. He had grown up with order and routine, the precision of shop hours and dinner bells and his father's ledgers lined up like soldiers on a shelf. But he hadn't grown up with this— mud on boots beneath the table, a baby squealing as he reached for someone's biscuit, hands flying to catch it before it tumbled into the butter dish. He hadn't known raised voices and boisterous laughter and a profound sense of belonging.

He hadn't known how much he needed it. All of it. But especially he hadn't known how much he needed Victoria.

"Are you hiding out here, Mr. Bernhardt?"

He turned and smiled as his wife stepped off the porch, her shoulders and arms wrapped in a shawl, her cheeks pink with pleasure. Her hair was pinned up with the usual neatness, though a few strands had escaped to dance in the breeze.

And she was beautiful. Radiant, really, in a way that defied explanation. His fingers itched for his paints and canvas. A familiar feeling.

"No, Mrs. Bernhardt. Not hiding." He reached for her hand. "I was observing the colts. They've made a game of kicking mud at each other."

She laughed softly, resting her head against his shoulder. "You're painting them in your mind, aren't you?"

He chuckled. She knew him so well. "I might have been." He could feel something different in the way she leaned against him—slightly more careful, more protective of the space between them. It was subtle, but he noticed. She'd been quieter this past week. Thoughtful. Something had changed but he wasn't sure what. Not something he feared. Just . . . different.

"Dinner was wonderful," she said.

"Mrs. Adler's roast or Amanda's pie?"

"Both." She smiled up at him. "Though I suspect your second helping of pie had more to do with pleasing Amanda than your actual appetite."

"You wound me, I daresay. I am a man of discerning tastes."

"You're a man who will eat anything with brown sugar and cinnamon in it."

He grinned as he tucked a strand of hair behind her ear. "I'm a man who thinks he may have found heaven on earth."

"Not quite that perfect."

"Near enough." He leaned in to kiss her forehead. Then, as she nestled closer, he rested his chin on the top of her head.

Across the open range, the evening light edged the Tetons with golden strokes.

"I'm glad you're happy," she said softly.

"I am happy. I'm home."

Home. It had taken him awhile to realize that he'd needed a home more than he'd needed freedom. And in finding his home, he'd discovered he was more free than ever before.

"It's not so much because of what I'm painting or where I'm painting or how much I'm painting," he said, more to himself than to her. "It isn't even because people are paying attention to my work more than ever before. It's that I wake up and want to paint what I see in this place. Not somewhere far off. Right here. These mountains. These people. You. Over and over and over again."

They stood in silence, the quiet wrapping around them like a prayer.

After a while, she shifted in his arms. "There's something I've been meaning to tell you."

He drew back so he could see her face. "Yes?"

Before she could answer, the sound of William's voice rang out from the porch. "Are you two going to stay out there all night? You'll freeze to death if you do. Besides, you're missing all the fun."

Victoria laughed and pressed a kiss to Roger's cheek. "I'll tell you later. It can wait."

THE FIRE in the bedroom had burned low, the embers casting a soft orange glow that danced across the walls. The sounds of laughter and clinking dishes had long since faded into the hush of night, leaving only the rustle of wind through the bare branches outside.

Victoria stood at the basin, brushing her hair with slow, thoughtful strokes. Roger had pulled back the quilt and settled into bed, one arm folded beneath his head, watching her with that quiet, steady look she loved so much.

This had been his room once—before October, before their wedding, before they'd made a home together in the little house near the school. Now it was only borrowed for the night. But still, it held a sort of comfort. A beginning. One of many.

He didn't speak as she finished brushing her hair, only held out his hand when she turned to him, inviting her near. She crossed the room, slipped beneath the quilt, and let herself lean against him, her head on his shoulder, her palm resting just above his heart.

"Did you mean it?" she asked softly.

He turned his face toward her, pressing a kiss into her hair. "Mean what?"

"What you said out by the pasture. About this being heaven on earth."

He gave a quiet chuckle. "Near enough."

She pulled back so their eyes could meet. She smiled but didn't laugh. Not this time.

"What?" he asked, sensing there was something still to be said.

"I've had a secret for a couple of weeks."

"A secret? From me?"

"I haven't told anyone."

He felt a sliver of alarm. "What?"

"I haven't told anyone, although someone else knows."

"Who?" His voice was louder this time.

"Dr. Grant."

Confusion made him frown.

At last she smiled. "I thought you might guess what that meant."

He shook his head.

Her fingers brushed the edge of his nightshirt. "Roger, darling, we're going to have a baby."

For a heartbeat, he didn't move. Then he shifted enough to see her face more clearly, searching her eyes. "Truly?"

She nodded. "I saw Dr. Grant earlier in the week. I've been waiting for the perfect moment to tell you. But tonight, when we were outside, I realized any moment I told you would be perfect."

His eyes shimmered, reflecting the firelight. "You're well?"

"I'm well. Just tired. A little . . . in awe, I suppose. And I keep wondering what kind of mother I'll be."

Roger brought her hand to his lips and kissed it, then laid it over his chest again. "You'll be the kind that teaches with kindness, sings lullabies in perfect pitch, and stands firm when the world tries to rattle you. The kind who will cross a country to make sure the child she loves is all right, the same way you did for the brother you love."

She swallowed hard, tears pricking the corners of her eyes. "And you? What are you thinking now?"

He smiled then. "I'm thinking I'll paint what I see.

And what I feel. And what I pray for. And I'll love the both of you with everything I am."

Silence settled around them again, soft and full.

Through the window, moonlight spilled across the floor, silver outlines on wooden planks. The fire let out a soft pop, as if affirming the moment with its own quiet benediction.

Victoria rested her hand over the flat of her belly and closed her eyes.

He was right. She'd crossed a country because of love, never imagining that an even greater love awaited her in this place. In a little town with a name she hadn't known at the time.

She'd come home. To a place where laughter lingered around the supper table, where roots grew deeper with every season, where love—steady and faithful—was more than enough.

And now, where a new life would begin.

The British Are Coming Series
Books 1 - 6

Available now.

Learn more on Robin's website.

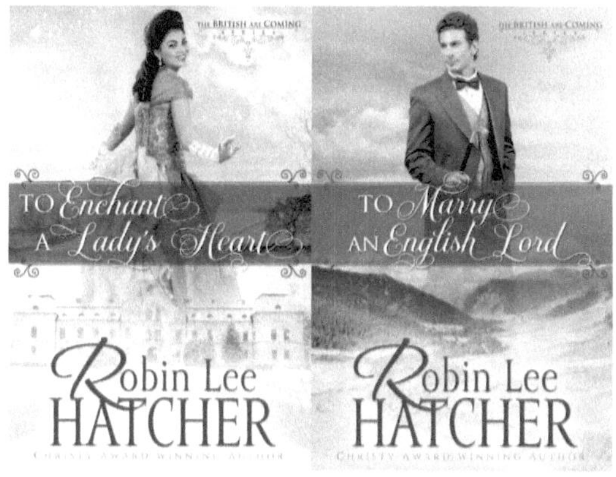

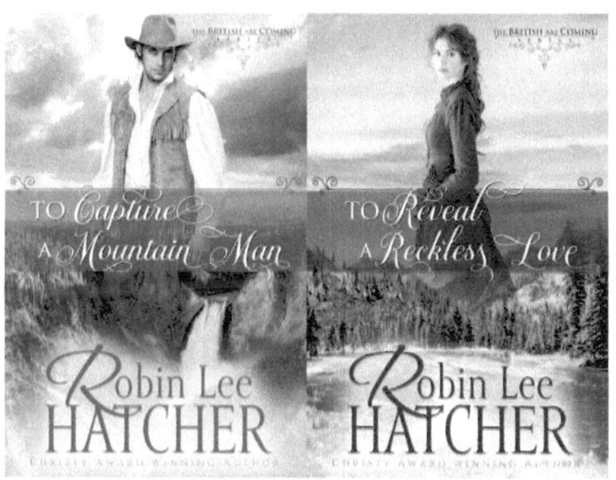

And coming in 2026 . . .

THE BRITISH ARE COMING
TO Find WHERE She Belongs
Robin Lee HATCHER
CHRISTY AWARD WINNING AUTHOR
THE BRITISH ARE COMING
TO Fall IN Love AT Christmas
Robin Lee HATCHER
CHRISTY AWARD WINNING AUTHOR

Robin Lee Hatcher is the best-selling author of over 95 books. Her well-drawn characters and heartwarming stories of faith, courage, and love have earned her both critical acclaim and the devotion of readers. Her numerous awards include the Christy Award, the RITA® Award, Romantic Times Career Achievement Awards for Americana Romance and for Inspirational Fiction, the Carol Award, and Lifetime Achievement Awards from both Romance Writers of America® (2001) and American Christian Fiction Writers (2014).

When not writing, Robin enjoys being with her family, spending time in the beautiful Idaho outdoors, Bible art journaling, reading books that make her cry, watching romantic movies, knitting, and decorative planning. A mother and grandmother, Robin makes her home on the outskirts of Boise, sharing it with a demanding Papillon dog.

Learn more about Robin and her books and subscribe to her newsletter on her website at robinlee hatcher.com

Also by
Robin Lee Hatcher

Stand Alone Titles

Like the Wind

I'll Be Seeing You

Words Matter

Make You Feel My Love

An Idaho Christmas

Here in Hart's Crossing

The Victory Club

Beyond the Shadows

Catching Katie

Whispers From Yesterday

The Shepherd's Voice

Ribbon of Years

Firstborn

The Forgiving Hour

Heart Rings

A Wish and a Prayer

When Love Blooms

A Carol for Christmas

Return to Me

Loving Libby

Wagered Heart

The Perfect Life

Speak to Me of Love

Trouble in Paradise

Another Chance to Love You

Bundle of Joy

The British Are Coming

To Enchant a Lady's Heart

To Marry an English Lord

To Capture a Mountain Man

To Reveal a Reckless Love

Boulder Creek Romance

Even Forever

All She Ever Dreamed

The Coming to America Series

Dear Lady

Patterns of Love

In His Arms

Promised to Me

Where the Heart Lives Series

Belonging

Betrayal

Beloved

Books set in Kings Meadow

A Promise Kept

Love Without End

Whenever You Come Around

I Hope You Dance

Keeper of the Stars

Books set in Thunder Creek

You'll Think of Me

You're Gonna Love Me

The Sisters of Bethlehem Springs Series

A Vote of Confidence

Fit to Be Tied

A Matter of Character

Legacy of Faith series

Who I am With You

Cross My Heart

How Sweet It Is

For a full list of books, visit robinleehatcher.com

www.ingramcontent.com/pod-product-compliance
Lightning Source LLC
Chambersburg PA
CBHW021236310726
48971CB00006B/1841